HELEN WITH A SECRET

and other stories

ALSO BY MICHAEL DELISLE IN ENGLISH
The Sailor's Disquiet (Translated by Gail Scott)

HELEN WITH A SECRET
and other stories

by Michael Delisle

Translated by Gail Scott

THE MERCURY PRESS

The publisher gratefully acknowledges the financial assistance of the Canada Council for the Arts and the Ontario Arts Council. The publisher further acknowledges the financial support of the Government of Canada through the Book Publishing Industry Development Program (BPIDP) for our publishing activities, and the Government of Ontario through its OTC program.

NOTES ON THE TEXT
The epigraph to the story "Helen with a Secret," a quotation from Jorge Luis Borges, is translated by Gail Scott. Asterisks denote text that was in English in the original French version of this book.

Edited by Beverley Daurio
Cover design by Gordon Robertson
Composition and page design by Beverley Daurio
Printed and bound in Canada
Printed on acid-free paper
1 2 3 4 5   06 05 04 03 02

Canadian Cataloguing in Publication Data
Delisle, Michael
[Helen avec un secret et autres nouvelles. English]
Helen with a secret and other stories
Michael Delisle : translated by Gail Scott
Translation of : Helen avec un secret et autres nouvelles.
ISBN 1-55128-100-7
I. Scott, Gail II. Title. III. Title: Helen avec un secret et autres nouvelles.
English.
PS8557.E4455H4413 2002   C843'.54   C2002-904581-9
PQ39192.D3435H4513 2002

The Mercury Press
Box 672, Station P, Toronto, Ontario Canada M5S 2Y4
www.themercurypress.ca

CONTENTS

FALLOW GROUND

for my brother
who's always around

TWO YEARS, DAY AFTER DAY, ALWAYS THE SAME THING

For two years, day after day, always the same old thing. I sit glued to the piano, on Mother's orders, and practise away. I may happen to find a musical passage that's simply astounding. Or I may find myself listening stunned to the genius of Bach. I may happen to yawn with boredom at the thought of running through the thirty-six scales, in major and minor, in chromatics, thirds, arpeggios, for the one-thousandth time, then starting all over again. Sometimes I may happen to hate the piano.

On top of the piano, I have to go to high school because at my age it's the law plus I'm in charge of housework at home because those were the first instructions Mother gave after the divorce. I'm sort of the live-in help. My brother does what he can.

Since the divorce, we've lived in a half-empty building, no janitor so no hope of having a clean entryway any day soon, in a neighbourhood of apartments that look like stacked boxes as far as your eye can see. What's funny about the buildings in our street is that the contractors, for obscure fiscal reasons, took off before the construction was finished. For example, our balcony, on the second floor, has no railing: it's nothing but a platform, a trampoline into empty space. The municipality, outraged at this state of affairs, is trying to exert pressure on the builders by refusing to complete the road work. Impeccable logic. Our street is made of packed earth like at the beginning of the century. With each swerve of a car, dust whirls into a cloud and our windows are deep beige. The rent is cheap.

The three of us are in a cramped five-room apartment: my older brother, me, and Mother, a divorced real estate agent in the prime of her thirties. Then there's my Uncle Richard who I always feel near, like a lucky star, since he died ten years back. He speaks into my left ear or into my right, asa the mood takes him, whispering little philosophical tips that make me suddenly dreamy, or else rude jokes that make me burst out laughing at the wrong time. From the outside, to people around me, I sometimes look like a retard lost in his own front yard, but I myself know I am all there.

My mother is fed up with everything since her divorce, including fed up with hearing about my ghost, and my brother stays mum when I try to tell him about it. For the family, the subject of my uncle has gradually become kind of taboo, and for me, Richard has slowly turned into a secret I carry here, deep in my heart.

MY BROTHER THE ARTIST

My brother has a gift. Already at six if you gave him a round piece of branch and a pocket knife, he coaxed a totem out of it, in ten minutes. At seven, fiddling with a lump of clay, he extracted a mermaid, a unicorn, a monster. Today, at sixteen, with fine wood, corrosive dyes and thin wire, he makes miniatures. A little table. A little buffet. A little cedar trunk. Concealing it from Mother, who would certainly disapprove of the badly lit work conditions, he strains his eyes late into the night to finish "turning" the bar of a high chair, or to polish with his thumb the side of a china cabinet. These days, he is working on the smallest chair in the world.

Often he doesn't know what day it is. To my way of thinking, this lack of awareness surrounds him with a sort of peaceful halo. I think it makes him seem nice. Not great to talk to. But nice. Needless to say, I am the one who takes care of the evening meal at home.

FRANCINE'S WAKE-UP CALL

Seven-thirty a.m. I grab my schoolbag and head at top speed down to the semi-basement, to the neighbour's in number two. I open the door without knocking and Grizzly, a pathetic aging poodle, greets me in silence. In the living room of number two little Remi, aged four, holds up a jar of Aunt Jemima syrup and pauses, ruminating something bad. His little sister Mona, two, is enthroned right in the middle of the sofa in a dune of cereal with a milk carton at hand. She's giggling so hard she's practically choking. The little devils ignore me, pursuing their misdemeanors.

I enter without knocking, like we agreed, into what apartment rental agents call the "master bedroom" and find, in the master bed, among the tangled sheets and flattened pillows, a very young redhead asleep with her mouth open, snoring lightly, and wearing a short cotton sweater with a faded, out-of-date *Keep on truckin'** slogan. I put my schoolbag down in the bedroom doorway and go sit beside her.

— Francine, it's seven-thirty, Francine, wake up! I say, gently shaking her shoulder.

— Hey, you look real handsome this morning, you, come closer, she murmurs, half asleep, extending a hand toward my hair.

— Francine, I tell her, Remi has spilt Honeycombs on the sofa and Mona's trying to fill every little Honeycomb hole with milk.

— Mona! she screams at the top of her voice.

At last, she sits up in bed, hugging her knees, and says, with a sidelong glance: "I give up, what 'm I gonna to do with 'em?" Her sadness— and this is what makes Francine brilliant— is as profound as it is passing. She looks at me abruptly, her lips twitching with a smile, pushing back her hair with her hand. Her laughing eyes are puffy.

— Give me your hand, I'm gonna make you touch something, she says in a lascivious voice.

— Francine, I'm gonna be late. You've got a huge pile of cleaning to do this morning... You're as bad as your kids, you know, I say, bursting out laughing.

— Give me a kiss, just a little *good morning*★ kiss, she asks me.

I quickly plant a peck her cheek and get up to go.

— Are you coming to wake me up tomorrow?

— If you want. Bye.

I race out at top speed. Pausing, on my way, to check what the kids are up to, I see Remi standing on a chair behind Mona, his arm out, about to pour syrup on the innocent head of his sister absorbed with filling up all the holes in the Honeycombs. I'm smart enough not to get involved. I exit, taking the stairs four at a time.

NANCY DUBREUIL-BOURQUE WANTS TO KILL ME

I rush out and, right in front of the apartment building door, run smack into Nancy Dubreuil-Bourque, wearing a safari suit under her beige trench coat. She's holding a bouquet of metal stakes under one arm and the key of her Cutlass Salon in her free hand. She points her key like a menacing spear, and with a firm, restrained voice issuing from between her pressed lips like sharp blades, she addresses me.

—You and I, she says, are going to have a talk. Right now, I haven't got time, but just you wait.

With a clatter, she throws the steel pickets into the trunk, immediately slamming it so hard I jump. She jumps into her burgundy Cutlass and takes off furiously. I get the impression she knows all about my "wake-up calls" to Francine's, the young mother in number two, and she's going to make me pay dearly for inappropriate intimacy. Nancy Dubreuil-Bourque is my mother. I know her well. These days, when she gets mad she is like a monster.

I pick up a bundle of VENDU-SOLD signs that she dropped in the mud in her rush to leave, and toss it onto our balcony. She hasn't needed any for quite a while, and I can tell by her mood, Dubreuil-Bourque won't be needing any today.

HEAVY FEET IN CLAY

It's raining. On the way to school, past the apartment buildings and before the shopping centre, come fields pockmarked with stranded excavations; fields studded with immobile cranes, with forlorn foundations. Lack of workers or lack of money, in any case, definitely something lacking. What floats over the construction sites, even more than the damp cold, is inertia. You might say the work has stopped because nothing made it go on. On top of that, it's raining.

I get an image of Nancy Dubreuil-Bourque with an armload of FOR SALE sign stakes. I see the en-garde position of her pointy key. I remember her threats. Very unfair threats if you ask me. But trouble is coming, because it's been a long time since Dubreuil-Bourque was willing to listen.

I walk in the gloopy clay mud. As a little kid, this boot suction noise used to make me laugh because it reminded me of slurping jello; now it depresses me because the heaviness weighing me down doesn't seem to be something that will go away like I used to naively think, but instead is a permanent fact of life. They will never finish these buildings! They will always be putting it off until later! And even if they were to finish, there would always be something to fix or repair and they would drag out these maintenance jobs the same way they drag out their lives. And so, as a result of letting things slide, chaos would take over again. I feel like there is no hope. The earth slurps every step I take like the fingers of death grasping at my ankles. It's twice as hard as usual to lift my feet. The walk to school seems interminable.

I stop. It's a cold rainy day. I stop to think up a reason for continuing to live in this dump. Something to make me go on. I can't think of a thing. My heart feels heavy. I sigh. Then my Uncle Richard's there, saying: "You are not alone."

He's right. What's really depressing is to be alone and I am not alone, my Uncle Richard is always with me. I start walking again. My rain boots weigh a ton. The residential complexes are ugly enough to make you puke. But I am not alone. I am not alone. How could I forget that?

"GOLD IS TENSILE"

I find madame Dacier's chemistry class a deadly bore, but the class is divided on the subject: half the kids religiously take down everything she copies onto the board from an old book of notes, while the other half— my half— spaces out if the class falls into an afternoon slot on the grid, or else nods off to sleep if it's a morning class. There are supposed to be questions at the end of the class, but we suspect madame Dacier's reasons for always postponing the question period to the next class, on the pretext there are too many notes to take down. That way we never get a chance to challenge her formulas. In fact, she could be a badminton specialist (name anything but chemistry) and nobody would be surprised. On my side of the room I daydream. I imagine the most horrible things, images of Nancy Dubreuil-Bourque, armed with her Cutlass key, saw-toothed, ready to disfigure me in a cruel act of revenge. As she moves toward me, her feet stamping out a heavy beat reminiscent of Godzilla, I kneel to beg forgiveness, but nothing is good enough, hysteria possesses her. Madame Dacier pauses in her copying.

— Does Monsieur Bourque wish to share his daydreams with us?

I shrug my shoulders, a little impudently.

— Don't tell me you are managing to pay attention! she marvels.

Immediately Richard can be heard in the hollow of my ear. "Tensile?" he asks. Without missing a beat I innocently toss out: "Tensile? Madame, what does that mean?"

— Tensile? she responds, disconcerted.

— Yes, you wrote "Gold is tensile" on the board. What does that mean, "tensile?"

Madame Dacier hesitates, shuffling around nervously through her notes. "Uh... it's slipped my mind," she mumbles to gain time. "Tensile... uh... " Already the sniggering can be heard from the rows of students. Students who usually ignore me congratulate me with the thumbs-up sign. Madame Dacier, embarrassed, says she'll come back to that next class; for the time being we still have a lot of notes to copy. From now on, I am willing to bet that Hélène Dacier will leave me alone.

OUR FIRST SONG

I haven't forgotten the first time I met Francine back at the beginning of the summer. She was often looking out her living-room window, which is right at ground level. Her then-platinum hair shimmered for the benefit of passers-by and she never failed to throw me a big smile when she saw me. We already knew each other by sight when she broke the ice.

— Are you coming in for a Seven-Up? she asked.
— Can't, I have to practise *The Hungarian Rhapsody* for next Saturday. I'm behind with my practising, I told her, completely straightforward.

Right away, I wondered why I had to go and say the title. A minute longer and I'd be singing the opening bars for her.

— Too bad, she said, eyeing with a small opportunistic smile the gape in my badly tucked-in sweater.

This girl was obviously after my body. Twenty-one with two kids already. Really, she was only seven years older than me, which would make her the same age as my mother when I got to be twenty-eight, and there's nothing terrible about that, per se... This line of thinking was making me nervous.

She tried again with a friendly "I'm Francine. And you?" "Me too," I replied in the politest voice I could muster, then ran to hide my red face.

VIRTUALLY NOTHING

In the shopping centre, between two shoe stores, is a video-game arcade where you can find all the kids who are skipping classes, or all the ones hanging out there before going home. The only other thing to do in this shopping centre (and therefore in this whole suburb), is to walk the mall. You start at Bonimart and you go all the way to Zellers. At Zellers, you have a choice: either go in and walk all around the store or head back to Bonimart.

There are benches in the centre of the mall. We park ourselves on them. The mall is the place where you smoke your first cigarettes, throat-burning and nauseating. A big simpleton of a guard comes over and says move on. "No loitering," he warns, indicating a sign that says NO LOITERING. Usually we make fun of him by saying something like: "Hey, he knows how to read!" Then we get up. We take a walk. As far as Bonimart.

In the video arcade, time doesn't exist. You get hypnotized by the luminosity of the screens. Even more insidious, you never get sick of those games. As soon as one round finishes, another starts, quicker than lightning, and it goes on like that until closing time.

LET'S SMASH SOMETHING TODAY

Last Sunday, the day the shopping centre is always closed, was weird.

In the field next to the abandoned construction site, some grade-eleven guys were forcing a young frog they found near a pool of water to smoke. One of the guys would pinch his lips shut around the filter to make him inhale. Forced laughter floated from the group. False laughter.

I hurried past. At first I felt horrified, thinking of the poor creature sweating its last tears, and then, gradually, guilty I hadn't tried to stop them... What a coward. Why are heroes only in stories? Why are games the only place people act brave? Why isn't it possible to be heroic right here and now, on this wretched earth. I heard Richard saying to me: "Your piano." I didn't know if he was ordering me to practise (I'm always behind with my practising) or offering me an enigmatic explanation for the absence of heroism in the lives of suburbanites. Richard practically always speaks in riddles.

What can I do since the frog is already dead? When I get home I'll play something like Massenet's *Elegy*. Or else a funeral march; I think I remember a beautiful one in the Beethoven sonatas, near the end of the exercise book. It's not much for a life I might have been able to save.

I STOP THE GOSSIP, AS BEST I CAN

My brother really wanted to stop lacquering the smallest chairback in the world and help me peel the potatoes. Between two strokes of the knife, he asks how Richard's doing. He's being ironic, so I am brief and to the point.

— Fine, I tell him, bluntly.

— Is it true that, with Francine... he ventures in an insinuating voice

— Francine, I tell him, to make everything perfectly clear, asked me to wake her in the morning before I leave for school because she has trouble waking up by herself.

— Did you do it with her? he asks with a leer.

Immediately I deny it. Then, after a moment's hesitation, and making him swear not to tell a soul, especially not Nancy Dubreuil-Bourque, I admit that once, in the hall, I brushed against her breasts. She could see how that disturbed me, so she lifted up her sweater and let me feel her up for around twenty minutes, the time it took to deprogram me from the initial trauma. I get all mixed up trying to explain while my brother kills himself laughing.

—You don't understand anything! I tell him angrily.

He's rolling on the floor, chortling hysterically.

LIGHTNING QUICK VISIT TO FRANCINE'S

My brother answers the phone, says "No problem" and hangs up at once.

— Mother will be half an hour late for supper, he says matter-of-factly.

That's enough time to make a quick trip to Francine's. I dash in, without knocking, and find her at the kitchen sink lathering the head of her poodle.

—You shampoo him! I blurt out, astonished.

—The kids glued his ears shut with cheese whiz. It dried. It's hard as a rock.

— Poor Grizzly, I say, with real sympathy, because he looks like he's crying.

— Later I'm dyeing my hair black, Francine announces.

— Oh yeah?

— A nice *blue-black,*★ she specifies, all happy with her great news. I just made up my mind. I've been *copper-red*★ for two months already... Funny eh, suddenly you think you have to be a redhead, being a redhead will change your life, but you get sick really fast of being a redhead... she explains, philosophically.

— Listen, Francine, my mother saw me leaving here this morning. I don't know what she thinks, but I have the feeling she'll be roaring mad when she gets home for supper. It's likely better I don't come visit any more.

— We never did anything wrong! she protests. You didn't want to either time.

— Yeah, I know. But when my mother gets mad you can't tell her a thing. It'll be okay in a while. Gotta get back up there.

— Hey, she breaks out suddenly, wait!

— What?

— Give me a kiss, she asks, wiping her hands on her apron.

I plant a rapid peck on her lips, and without missing a beat, she forces her tongue in my mouth, pleased with herself for playing this trick on me.

— Francine, I say, backing away.

She laughs a little. Suddenly I hear the door of my mother's Cutlass slam violently shut. My mother has a way of slamming a door, like nobody else.

— My God... I say, terrified.

— Take the fire escape up the back! says Francine quickly.

THE SUPPER HOUR

Nancy Dubreuil-Bourque's dictatorial silence lies heavily over the whole supper hour. We feel her anger heating up inside to the boiling point. After dessert, after what seems like a whole day, she asks my brother to leave us alone. "I have something to discuss with your brother," she says through gritted teeth. My brother is only too happy to go shut himself up in the quiet of his bedroom with the tiniest chair in the world.

— Do you know that woman is married? starts my mother, getting straight to the point.

— For one thing, I don't think she is or she would have told me and furthermore nothing has happened, I reply calmly.

— Impudent! she thunders, go to your room! I'll teach you how to talk to your elders! she screams at the top of her voice.

I get up.

— Sit! I'm not finished!

I sit down again.

— What would you say if instead of going out to earn our living, I threw in the towel? Do you think I'm having a good time? No I am not! Try to put that in your head...

My Uncle Richard irrelevantly advises going to bed.

— I have no choice but to punish you, she starts again. You are grounded for a month, do you hear? As soon as school's out, you come straight home. No more shopping centre, no more... (she stops and thinks). No more shopping centre, do you hear?

I go back to my room, sheepishly. Suddenly, maybe at Richard's prompting, I start laughing to myself as I remember her trying to enumerate all our local social and cultural activities. In this part of the world, there is, as a matter of fact, nowhere to go but the shopping centre. What a life!

SMALL FUGUE

My head bent over my piano keys, I feel sad and at loose ends. I concentrate on the small details, like my brother does. I stick my nail into a crack on the piano case. I run my finger along the black keys. I have never understood why my sharp keys get sticky quicker than my white ones. On the keyboard, there is a flake of paper from an old piece of sheet music russeted by decades; I pick it off. Grounded for a month. But where does she think I am supposed to go in my free time?

Suddenly, Richard says: "Play for me." And I assault a Bach fugue. A simple fugue, perfect in its beauty.

SURPRISE PHONE CALL

Nancy Dubreuil-Bourque goes out to buy some women's magazines. Two seconds later, Francine, apparently on the lookout since I warned her, calls me up. I am really glad to hear her voice. I can't stand Dubreuil-Bourque and I intend to disobey her because it's all she deserves. As a matter of fact, I was thinking of going to Francine's tonight. There's a horror film on channel ten. It'll cheer me up. But before I manage to put my plan into words, Francine informs me, in a whispering voice, that her husband the miner, who's been up in Greenland on a job for eight months, came home sooner than expected, this afternoon. He's a big guy, tough, muscular and insanely jealous. As I might have guessed, she's asking me not to come and wake her up in the morning any more. She has to hang up, because he's heading toward the kitchen and he's been drinking.

So I listen to *The Massacre of the Living Dead* by myself in the living room, catching cries of horror, from time to time, coming from Francine's place, below.

A FEW DAYS LATER...

On the way to school, the mud is still soft and gloopy and the earth sucks on my boots like the hands of the dead, grabbing me by the ankles. Still a cold rain falling. Picking up my feet takes so much effort I feel like crying.

It almost worries me how, for the past month, the weather has remained the same. Stagnation has always seemed to me an unnatural state; change, or at least movement, was a law of nature.

Maybe what goes for nature doesn't go for the suburbs...

DUBREUIL-BOURQUE DOESN'T LAY OFF

Nancy Dubreuil-Bourque scolds for nothing. She accuses me of carelessly throwing away telephone messages from her clients. In the heat of the argument, I tell her I never did but it's not a bad idea. She slaps me. I take it without a word, but if looks could kill. She yells, shaking her clenched fists at the ceiling. Scenes of everyday life.

Nancy Dubreuil-Bourque is visibly paranoid these days. Every speck of dust turns into a plot hatched to make her mad and every coincidence (me going to the bathroom when she was thinking of going), a plot to make her crazy. It's not unusual these days to get an evil eye at dinner if the mine-strone is too salty, a fork thrown down on a plate for peas not heated enough, an accusatory ear-splitting "You're doing it on purpose!" for an overcooked meatball (Mater takes rare). On one recent unforgettable evening, my brother and I kept staring at each other, without knowing, like the song says, whether to laugh or cry: Nancy Dubreuil-Bourque'd cracked the doorframe slamming the door because there was scum on the tapioca.

MY BROTHER OFFERS ME THE SMALLEST PIECE OF ADVICE IN THE WORLD

My brother is maybe the only person capable of understanding me. He knows like I do from experience how hard Mother is. I go to him, the one human being who can truly understand what a burden I have to bear, and complain. I always pick a moment when he is using a spindly pair of pliers with intense concentration. He's not listening. I leave his room. Nobody wants to listen to me. Nobody understands me. I'll be glad when I'm forty. Where in the world is Richard? It's the second time this week he's left me in the lurch when I need him. I go back to my brother again.

— If you were in my place, what would you do about her? I ask right out.

— Francine?

— No. I am not referring to Francine, I am referring to your mother, I tell him.

— Just put it out of your mind, he says without looking up from screwing in a dowel.

FRANCINE LEAVES US FOR ALBERTA

On my way home from school, I climb the apartment steps with lead feet. Suddenly I think I hear noises coming from Francine's. I hear sounds as clearly as if her door were open. I walk down to the semi-basement to have a look. She's there, wrapping a vase in newspaper. The living room is strewn with boxes.

— You're moving! I exclaim.

— Oh hi. Yeah. Next week. We're taking the kids and going. Henri found a job out there. That's where his parents are...

Each new revelation is delivered with a hint of uneasiness. She is embarrassed by my presence.

— What happened to your arm? I ask, pointing to a giant bruise.

— Henri's in a bad mood since he came back from the mines.

— What are you going to do?

— I told ya, we're moving to Alberta. We're gonna have a whole bungalow all to ourselves.

She closes the box, crossing the flaps.

— Are you going to miss me? she asks, simpering.

— Francine, you've got a broken tooth, I tell her in a real worried voice.

— It's just a little piece that came off. Stop bothering yourself about me, she says, suddenly cool.

She smiles at me, tells me I am a nice guy and she will always have good memories of me. I will never see her again.

FINALE

For the last fifteen minutes Nancy Dubreuil-Bourque's accusations have turned into downright insults. Her tone of voice, more or less explosive, has drawn my brother from his room. He is standing near the kitchen where the confrontation is taking place.

Nancy Dubreuil-Bourque has made one insult too many and I raise my right arm to hit her in the face, when, for the first time since my Uncle Richard has been in contact, I feel his hand grab my arm. Up to now, Richard has always made his presence felt by enigmatic hints, ambiguous axioms or calming musical phrases running through my head; very occasionally, when he was extremely close, I felt a rush of heat on my back at the level of my heart. But this is the first time that I have felt the power of his grasp on my arm. Seeing it stop moving in mid-air, Dubreuil-Bourque breaks into a superior mocking smile. She taunts me: "You couldn't if you wanted to. You wouldn't dare…"

Then Richard murmurs very clearly: "There's no reason for you to stop, but you will anyway. Go on! I'm with you." Instantly I draw my hand back towards my body, and lifting a finger, I say coolly to my mother: "You're wrong, I am capable of a lot and I am going to prove it to you right now. I am going to tell you something and you are going to listen." I take a step forward and her smile is immediately wiped off her face. I am two inches from her face. My boldness surprises and disconcerts her.

I explain to her with a calm as formidable as it is sudden that I love her and I will always love her. Neither the mean things she can do, nor the nasty things she can say, *nothing in her power* will make me change my mind. Either she will take twenty years to get used to it, or she will get used to it at once, but, I tell her, one way or the other, she will have to face up to it sooner or later.

I take a step forward and she takes a step back. Nancy Dubreuil-Bourque is totally disarmed. The ball is in my court and I don't do a thing. I have decided the war is over. My control over the situation has my brother gaping. He watches the scene completely subdued. Never, since the divorce, has our mother been so taken aback. Barely controlling her tears, she withdraws to her room without saying a word. She closes her door like a normal person.

A LITTLE UNEASINESS IN OUR NEW ORDER

Nancy Dubreuil-Bourque scratches on my door with her fingernails and comes into my room while I am tinkling away at a Diabelli andante. She hardly knows where to start. I can feel Richard restraining himself from whispering anything in my ear. Maybe there is nothing to say. Maybe what needs to be said is beyond words, can only be shown by gestures, musical notes or even body language. Mother seems to be in a state of near stupor since our big argument. I smile when I remember my arm stopped not a minute too soon by my uncle as I was about to hit my own mother. God, how terrible.

My mother says: "Keep on playing. It's beautiful." And she moves back without kissing me. She remains at a distance. A hug would maybe be in order, but she doesn't touch me. We're not that kind of family.

— You're quite advanced for your age, she observes, stepping slightly forward again.

— It's not so much me, but Richard.

— Don't tell me you're still into that... she says, as gloomily as if she had just found out I was still sucking my thumb.

— He's there! I feel it, I hear him, I say, getting carried away.

— Okay, okay, she says, to calm me down. You are a strange child, she finishes in a low voice, seriously puzzled.

Our smiles show how tired we are.

HARD GROUND

The ground is starting to freeze. It will be easier to walk over on the way to school. It's colder. Cold is good. It keeps you alert.

In the field, the snow will fall like a benediction on the disorder of those abandoned constructions.

Earlier, in my room, I was lying to my mother. I no longer feel Richard's presence.

I GET A PRESENT

My brother comes to sit beside me in the living room and hands me a little black lacquered cardboard box that he made himself from a shoe box.

— Open it, he says.

— What is it?

— Open it, you'll see.

I open the box. Inside is a four-inch violin, painted mahogany. Every detail is perfect.

— It's a present, he explains.

— You made that! I exclaim, impressed.

— It took me two weeks.

The instrument is so finely crafted it takes your breath away. The bridge fastidiously perpendicular, the sound holes perfectly formed, the hollow side panels, the violin pegs; everything's there, including three threads of pale copper to serve as strings.

— Does it play? I ask naively.

— No, he replies, a little sadly.

— But it doesn't matter, I add hurriedly, it's incredible. Really incredible.

— It would have required more stress, the wood's too fragile.

With a blissful expression glued on my face, I study the masterpiece. My brother is proud of his gift. I am proud of my brother.

—Why a violin? I ask him, to relieve the emotional tension.

— Because you take piano lessons, he answers, all pleased.

Seeing that I totally fail to grasp the connection, a fact I awkwardly try to conceal by nodding my head attentively, he explains: "Piano, violin, it's all music."

— That's true, I say, relieved.

My brother is a genius. The instrument he has made for me is truly high art! It is disturbing to think that right here, in this hideous and boring suburb, there is an inspired genius like him, creator of fascinating marvels, and that this genius dedicated to the expression of beauty is my brother. That he is around every day. That he is there for me. That he gives me gifts of inestimable value! How can I ever repay him? I don't know.

RICHARD'S LAST WORDS

There are old truck ruts in the frozen mud. In the little tracks in the earth, the remaining water has turned into white panes of glass, thin and frost-trimmed.

My Uncle Richard often used to say to me: "The love of gardens," or "The love of gardening," pointing to this fallow ground. I wonder what garden he was talking about. Here is nothing but desolation and all the people living here are resigned to it. What gardening? I don't get it.

Richard used to say to me sometimes: "I won't always be here. Of what use will a good star be to you once the sun has risen?" I didn't really pay attention. Living without Richard was unthinkable His mysterious presence made my life less banal.

I am going to miss my uncle's riddles.

I walk until I reach the main road. The sky is low. It is a bittersweet day like so many others, except my heart feels fuller. Not enough to change my life. But enough to give a little to the next person who asks.

1991

PRAYERS FOR EDMOND

Edmond Bourcier and Pit Côté have had a few. They totter towards the boat. They are going fishing for ouananiche.[†] Behind them glimmer the blue and yellow lights of Saint-Coeur-de-Marie, the fields of ripe hay. It's a cool August night. A night with a breeze on a lake as wide as a sea.

The Moon wanes.

They always do this. Weekends, after a few drinks, Edmond and Pit go off to row around the lake and fish ouananiche. Edmond carries the beer and Pit rows. At the helm, Pit will tell stories or sing songs, and Edmond, his appreciative audience slumped in the stern, will listen with a smile. The two fishermen have neither rod, nor hook, nor bait, nor net. At some point, one of them is going to pretend to be surprised. They always have a good laugh.

Pit Côté whistles as he walks. He's a compact twenty-eight-year-old man with solid gait; he compensates for being short with a slightly overblown tenor.

His arms are powerful. In fifteen minutes, his friend Edmond will be enjoying a good view of the lights of Saint-Coeur-de-Marie.

[†] a Montagnais term for landlocked salmon

As he puts his foot in the boat, Edmond lurches and Pit grabs him by the arm, crying "Jeez, Ed, you're going to make us sink before we leave the dock." He bursts out laughing. That gets Edmond laughing, too.

Edmond puts the case of beer in the wet bottom of the rowboat, muttering, as if to himself, that a little lake water will keep the beer cool. Pit takes the oar, and with his hand cupped to his mouth like a blow-horn, he bellows "Anchors away!" to Saint-Coeur-de-Marie.

There is a good swell on the lake. Its surface is too vast to remain flat. Edmond says it is an ocean. He keeps to the back. Like a child. He runs his fingers over the water. He watches the shore grow smaller. On a night in 1959.

— Hey, Pit! the water's warm, says Edmond, slurring a little. Edmond is happy.

Mirande's kitchen is extraordinarily clean. There, morning, noon and nights, she kneels on a tasselled cushion, before a chair she uses as a prie-dieu. It is a slow, painful, difficult exercise.

She pulls her white chignon tighter.

Since she turned eighty, her body has considerably shrunk; the solid young farm woman has withered into a delicate old shell. Her bones are frail, her skin transparent. She crosses herself and kisses the cross of her dark red rosary. She folds her emaciated hands and brings them up to her chin. She says her prayers, exhaling gently on knuckles traversed by a dark vein, like a black worm on the bone.

Her sweater wrapped shawl-like around her shoulders, Mirande prays. On her knees in front of her chair, she bows her head and a long strand escapes from her chignon.

She whispers, "In the name of the Father, the Son, and the Holy Ghost. Amen."

She sighs. To feel it deep in her soul.

Rowing along, Pit sings, "When a man takes up booze, it's because of a dame..." Dreamily, Edmond lets his hand skim along above the dark water.

The Moon is almost black.

It is a slightly windy night. Edmond, wet with sweat, has his shirt open. His black hair is greasy, and the circles under his eyes are reddened by liver spots. The sun was boiling hot today.

Edmond remembers the strong grip of his friend. Getting into the boat, Edmond staggered, and when Pit grabbed him by the arm he must have held him tight. Edmond remembers, with his cheek pressed down on his shoulder, his eyes vague...

Edmond is reminiscing.

*

It was a sticky July day, two years ago. He was emptying out a box of canned tomatoes at his brother's grocery store. Pit came in, tanned black and laughing. He had a voice you couldn't help noticing. It was the height of July and sweat dripped off him everywhere. He wanted cold beer and canned salmon. Edmond had fetched it from the back. Pit had put a friendly hand on his shoulder and started to tell him a story: "There were these two Indians, hey, who were goin' out huntin'. The one guy said to the other, he said... " Edmond had laughed so uncontrollably, his stomach hurt. On the badly shaved throat of the guy telling the story, sweat was falling in generous drops towards the tan-line at the edge of his under-shirt.

Edmond was charmed.

His fingers graze the water. It is a night in 1959, and Saint-Coeur-de-Marie is growing smaller.

Mirande is praying, murmuring, whispering, revelling a little in *the fruit of your womb is blessèd*. Mirande prays to the dull clicking of clock hands. Those on the console of the electric stove, those on the wind-up alarm clock, those on the clock on the wall lording it over the two others: a superb gift from her son Maurice.

The counter gleams. The chrome of the kitchen set has been polished. Chair and table legs, washed underneath. The refrigerator purrs. There is a hint of creosote in the air.

Her cocoon's sweet freshness, winter and summer alike.

Mirande prays for unmarried mothers. For delinquents. For Esther Tremblay and her husband Paul-Henri. For the two sisters Léonie and Année Bouchard. For Nazaire, Roland, Fernand and Nicole. Laure and her son Théo. Eugène Philie and his brother André.

Mirande prays that the innocent souls of Lise, Mariette, Josephe, Gaetane, Jean-Paul and Midas, the children she lost in infancy, may rest in peace. Josèphe was two days old. A puny one. She never made a sound. Midas was one-and-a-half. She sees Midas's eyes light up at the sight of a blancmange.

Mirande prays for her living children. Thérèse and her husband Edouard and their children Lison, Gisèle, Raymond and Louis. Raynald and his wife Hélène and her son Gaétan. Annette and her husband Jean-Jules who have no children. Maurice and his wife Hortense and their children Jean-Guy, Marie-Andrée, Jocelyne and Michel. André and his second wife Paula and her children Gaston and Guylaine. Yvon and his wife Joyce, who live in the States, and their children Bobby and Philippe.

To each and every one, Mirande sends the blood-red flames of love that emanate from her heart.

And Mirande prays for her youngest son. A minute of silence for Edmond to be guided in his choices.

Dear God, what is to be done with Edmond?

Pit's expecting it. At a certain point, just when Saint-Coeur-de-Marie looks like a little fire flickering beyond the tiny islands, it never fails, Edmond stands up in the boat, stretches his arms to the sides and starts howling invocatory sounds that rhyme with nothing, cries of joy in a rather loose Montagnais. Edmond is not steady on his feet. His boat-stomping dance is dangerous. Pit keeps an eye on him.

He downs a beer and tosses the empty bottle overboard, as far as he can.

— Edmond! he cries. We forgot the fishing rods.

Edmond bursts out laughing. He laughs ridiculously hard, his shoulder shaking. It's the ouananiche fishing ritual. You forget the rods. You have a good laugh. You drink. You horse around on the lake with the village in the distance. All alone. Away from the world. Drinking in peace, rocked by the lake.

Mirande has a vision. More like a memory. Edmond, the scrawny one, is being carried by Maurice into the kitchen. Edmond at the age of thirteen had had a fainting spell, over-tired from helping with the haying. The sun was burning hot.

The Bourciers had a decent farm. Eight hectares of hay. About thirty egg-layers and a few cud-chewers.

Raynald and Maurice threw up the bales that André and Yvon piled on the trailer; Bourcier senior drove. Even Annette got involved. It was agreed that Edmond, a sickly child, didn't have to help. But on that particular day, his heart pounding with enthusiasm, Edmond had wanted to help. And the sun had pounded down on his head.

Edmond felt faint.

When he awoke in the kitchen with his mother who was slapping his cheek and his brother Maurice who was looking at the floor, Edmond had cried out that he was hungry. There was panic in his eye as he said it. He repeated, "I'm hungry, I'm hungry, I really am," as if afraid they wouldn't believe him. Mirande concluded he hadn't eaten enough.

Pit likes Edmond a lot. First of all, Edmond's a good drinker. And then, Edmond's a good audience when Pit gets going with his stories. He really listens.

— You like water, my good Ed?

Edmond strokes the surface of the water. He says water is magic.

— That reminds me of the story of Blaise Journet, the storyteller interjects.

Happily, Edmond looks up at him again. His friend always tells fish stories and already he's laughing.

— Why are you laughing, it's not funny. It's a true story!

— With a name like Blaise Journet? asks Edmond, in disbelief.

— It's a French name, from France, explains Pit, convincingly.

The storyteller admits he maybe sometimes exaggerates, but he swears this story is nothing but the truth: articles have been written about the accident. Roland Tremblay showed him one.

Pit pulls in one oar and Edmond opens two cool ones. He hands one to Pit and listens to the sad story of young Blaise Journet, a fifteen-year-old apprentice working for a large glass works in the south of France.

Blaise Journet was a glass blocker. Pit describes what a glass blocker does by means of gestures, using an oar to imitate the gesture of stirring molten glass. He compares the liquid mass to a monstrous soup. Glass-poling, he resumes, is like stirring the soup, in glass-making language.

Edmond is convinced by Pit's scientific knowledge. Each time pulverized glass is added, Pit pounds down with his oar in the boiling mass to make the bits melt easier. Everything leads one to believe that Blaise Journet was careless because, even though attenuated by a system of chains and pulleys, the stirring pole knocked him head first into the melting pot. The young boy fell into the molten glass; he disappeared in the bubbling broth.

The impact caused an infernal racket. A sulphurous cloud twisted towards the factory ceiling. The foreman immediately gave the command to put the fire out under the melting pot and a volunteer was called to pull out the body of young

Blaise before the mass solidified. Young Hervé de Monticul‡ stepped forward.

— Pit! entreats Edmond, quit putting me on.

Pit continues, a smile playing at the corners of his mouth.

By the time the soup had cooled enough, young Blaise Journet had completely disappeared. Even when they spread out the paste, there was no sign of him. Not even a trace of spleen. The child had been calcinated, dispersed, made transparent.

Edmond's mouth is hanging open.

— Nothing? he asks.

— Not a speck! iterates Pit. Completely evaporated. His ashes dissolved instantly.

Pensive, Edmond says that must be like falling into the sea. The sea swallows everything you throw it. All the drowned people, the shipwrecks, the broken masts, dead crabs, fish guts, empty bottles, everything vanishes. With the passing years, everything ends up dissolving, salting the water. Edmond claims sea water is salty because of all the drowned people.

— You're not going to get depressed on me tonight! admonishes Pit.

‡ Monticul— literally mon 'ti-cul, or my little asshole

49

Mirande prays. For prisoners. For abandoned women. For widowers and widows. For orphans. For alcoholic men and alcoholic women. Mirande prays for the strength to accept that none of her children have taken the cloth.

She brings the rosary to her thin lips.

Mirande so wanted to offer one of her children to God's service. This is where she has failed.

Edmond would have made a perfect priest. A sensitive man, a little delicate. He hadn't what it took to take over the farm. He wasn't made to live off the land.

He would have been handsome in a black soutane.

Edmond suddenly stands up in the boat, and, with his arms flung out at the sides, he starts crying "Ayaah!" while tossing his head and pounding his feet, like Indians do.

Pit grabs him by the behind and, cursing and swearing, plunks him down on his seat. He's not in the mood for Edmond's outbursts. He lectures him on his recklessness.

Pit is afraid of madness.

Sitting back, calmed, his hand dragging in the water, Edmond is remembering a scene with his brother Maurice.

When he was thirteen, one day when the sun was boiling hot, Edmond offered to help with the haying. This was very unusual and his older brothers and his sister Annette teased him relentlessly. The needling quickly degenerated into a tussle. Edmond was having fun rolling in a haystack.

In the pushing and shoving, a bear-hug by Maurice, already a man, troubled Edmond, who fainted as he felt his burning cheek slide down Maurice's salty torso, against his musky odour, his violent peppery underarms. Edmond-the-pale had bowed down before all that animal glory.

Edmond wanted to die.

Maurice carried his young brother in his arms up to the house. He set him down on a chair, protesting he hadn't done it on purpose. Mirande still gave him a talking-to and Thérèse the eldest sister made everyone bread and molasses.

During the following days, Edmond wandered around. He walked along the bank, between the road and the lake, halting meditatively opposite the little islands, breathing in the smell of the water. Edmond was trying to name the thing that troubled him.

To calm the nagging voice in his mind, he suddenly stood up, throwing his arms out like a cross, and challenged God to give him a sign. He said, in the tone of a son speaking to a father, that he would commit his life to Him and Him alone if he found a gold coin. Right here and now. From no matter where, of no matter what mintage, with no matter what face. He wanted magic. A piece of gold. Just one. And Edmond made his wish.

When he opened his eyes, he saw a bright disk stuck in the sand a few feet from where he stood. It glinted. Terrified, he ran home.

Hunkered down in his bed, he began to feel afraid of his formidable conjuring powers. The obsession took on maniacal proportions. Since whatever he envisioned immediately appeared, he cultivated a terror of picturing any thing at all. The more inhuman the restrictions he tried to impose on his thinking, the more guilty thoughts multiplied in his suffering soul. He suffered in his very flesh. He suffered from the proximity of his brothers who were shamelessly turning into men and his sisters who were blossoming forth. He suffered from the nearness of the farm animals, free of all moral constraints. The mare with her wet folds, proffered. The stallion with his immeasurable member.

As soon as he realizes physical exercise is the best antidote to his runaway imagination, he starts working like a beast of burden. Bails of hay, cords of wood, shovels of earth. Earthly things to break apart, for ever breaking apart matter. For a while, he keeps up the pace; in moments of repose, he dreams up complex fragmentations. For a time, Edmond Bourcier has the blistered hands of a farmer. When night falls, he pays no attention to the magnificent arch above; he sits on the gallery and parses abstract categories before falling into a comatose sleep.

It didn't last. Eventually, Edmond became, once more, "the one who will not be a priest."

Edmond is a drinking man. On occasion, he works at his brother Maurice's grocery store.

At the age of thirty-five, Edmond Bourcier is a bachelor who lives with his mother and goes for boat rides on the lake with his friend Pit when he's had a few.

Mirande crosses herself and gets up very slowly, her hands gripping the chair. One knee then the other. Her father confessor has often assured her that at her age, she could pray sitting or lying down. Mirande is stubborn: a prayer is said on one's knees. Sitting or lying down, no blessing will be forthcoming.

In front of her electric stove, she heats a small glass of red wine with a pinch of cinnamon and a spoon of sugar. On very low heat.

Through the window, above her sink, Mirande notices the twinkling of a star in the black sky, and as if by magic, she remembers the priest at Saint-Irénée who, to the stupefaction of everyone, took his orders at the ripe age of forty.

Mirande's heart beams. She thanks the Lord on high for giving her hope. All is not lost for Edmond.

Not shaking more than usual, she empties the hot concoction into a sherry glass.

She puts on her nightgown while the sweetened wine grows lukewarm on the table. She takes her time. She returns to her chair and sips her mulled wine. She can't stop thinking about the priest from Saint-Irénée who became a priest at forty.

She smiles at the Sacred Heart nailed above the door.

She will sleep well, her head full of Edmond in moments of inspiration. They are a sign.

Edmond has been known to be inspired.

Edmond is snivelling. Pit, crushed, gives him a talking-to. He says life is too beautiful to cry over. You have to be happy.

Edmond looks at the black water, the awesome water. He says the water is soft this evening. He dips in his hand and brings a few drops up to his face. He breathes in the smell of the lake.

Water gives life. Water brings death. Life. Death. Water gives and takes back. Like a monotonous lullaby.

Pit rubs his ears. The lake air is freezing. He says they did-n't forecast such cold weather.

Murmuring almost inaudibly, Edmond explains, leaning over the waves, that a liquid mass spared Blaise Journet from his destiny. What would he have become without that accident? What would have become of Blaise Journet without the boiling glass? He would have become a fat man in an undershirt listening to Edith Piaf while eating crusty bread and drinking red wine. Instead, he is a window pane in a chateau with turrets and religious banners, he's a mirror in a museum full of round full-hipped statues, he's a ball the size of an apple containing a village under water snowing down.

Edmond's eyes look crazy; he sees each thing passing as he names it.

—You could say it has never been so dark, says Pit, a little worried.

The Moon is a suspended thread disappearing behind a cloud.

Edmond says that he understands boats. Water draws you because earth is base. Earth is the den of all iniquity. He repeats the water feels soft.

—We're going back, Edmond, Pit announces, my ears are starting to ache. The air is starting to freeze.

Pit keeps his head bowed, lost in thought. He clamps his hands over his ears to warm them up.

Mirande leaves her empty glass on the bedside table. She deposits a kiss on a pewter cross that she always has close at hand. She turns off her lamp. The pillow is plumped. The catalogue quilt is thick and tightly sewn. Mirande Bourcier likes to say that, to sleep well, the covers have to be heavy.

In the wee hours, when Edmond comes in, Mirande will open one eye. A tiny little bit. The batting of an eyelid. Trying as hard as he can not to make any noise, Edmond will nonetheless bump into a kitchen chair and burst out laughing. Mirande will smile a little and will fall back asleep reassured.

And she will have a kind thought for the priest from Saint-Irénée.

It is night over the lake below Saint-Coeur-de-Marie. The cloud has floated by. The stars have come out again. The Moon is a thin thread. Tomorrow, the night will be as black as slate. And if the sky is clear, it will be powdered with dazzling stars.

With his hands gripping the edge of the boat, Pit Côté screams his friend's name at the top of his lungs. His spent voice echoes over the lake. His friend Edmond must have slipped into the deep lake. With his hands covering his ears, to warm up his head, Pit wouldn't have heard a thing. Edmond would have spilled over the side with the roll of the swell. Like a ballast bag suddenly leaking its sand, Edmond has slid silently into the lake.

When Pit raised his head and wiped his eyes, he was alone. Now he screams the name of his friend out over the lake.

Edmond does not resurface and the visibility is zero.

Pit begs Edmond to say where he is. He says it's time to return to dry ground. Standing up in the boat, Pit spreads out his arms and, in a fanatic voice, he begs Edmond to come back.

Blissfully, Mirande sleeps.

Sleep radiates from Mirande.

The Moon is about to disappear.

Pit Côté plunges his arm into the lake and calls Edmond, sobbing. He looks for him, groping with his hands, in the water, black as ink.

1995

JANE SOUCY

You dance in place of the dead.

The children have stuck a witch on her broom on the window. She casts a joyous black shadow with a beautiful orange pumpkin under her arm. I take a close look at the carefully cut-out silhouettes. The children have been working hard.

Outside, in the park, there are almost no more leaves on the trees. The scene carries me off in a daydream.

Sitting very straight, Jane tells my mother a story. She stops in the middle of her sentence and, looking me straight in the eye, declares: "I know you don't like me." Then continues her anecdote, without missing a beat.

Nobody takes any notice. My mother is there, but I seem to be the only one who's heard. I don't know what to say; I don't think my Aunt Jane expects a reply: she tossed off the observation, flatly, and changed the subject. Continuing her story. I watch my mother fiddling with her car keys while listening to her sister.

I am a little offended. I believe I have always liked Jane. At least, it seems to me I have. I even used to like to say— it was our little greeting ritual— that she was my favourite aunt. But as soon as she said that, as soon as she interrupted what she was telling my mother (something about menstrual periods dragging on) to look me right in the eye and say, "You, my boy, don't like me," I felt uncomfortable because, deep down, she might be right.

When I think of Jane, I see her as a vamp behind her immense picture window on the shore of Little Lake Magog. And I see her with her very own peculiar habit, permanently impressed on my mind: she is nibbling on little pinched-off bits of raw hamburger. Sometimes she even carries a little ball of it wrapped in cellophane in her purse. The red taste of raw meat turns her on.

When I think of Jane I think of her deep cough. Before going to work, her husband slaps her upper back to loosen the mucus in her bronchial tubes. She calls it her "clapping." The exercise has been repeated every day since part of her lungs was removed.

When I think of Jane, when I think of her in my favourite way, she is a fortyish woman, in high seventies dudgeon, looking out at Little Lake Magog on a summer's evening. The lake looks strange. The fabric dye discharge from the textile factory has created a greeny-grey slick. The Chinese lanterns at the Roys' and the Coolidges' places reflect on its opaque surface. When dusk falls, just before darkness, the Chinese lanterns light up and Jane Soucy slips into something comfortable, low-cut and pale blue— something in a diaphanous material trimmed with soft feathery stuff around the wrists and neck— and she walks back and forth in front of her sweeping living-room window, a window that covers the whole wall, from the ceiling to the ankles. A show window. Her daughters are in bed. Her husband, Constable Soucy, is working late.

For people who live by the lake, the sight of Jane Soucy, alone in the living room, is nothing unusual.

In her show window, Jane is a powder blue form moving lazily, a neat Scotch sparkling orange in her left hand and a long cigarette between her fingers. Sometimes, she lovingly caresses her perfect breasts, delighting in the weight of the contour, the perkiness of the nipple.

You'd think she was dancing. She oscillates. She throws back her long black hair with a grand toss of the head. She closes her eyes and sways in her huge window, in front of the dead lake that at this hour of the day, takes on surreal tones.

She remains there until she hears her husband's car pull into the garage.

Like all fairly big lakes, Little Lake Magog has a monster that lives in its depths and a ghost who strolls, bloated by a tale of pathos, along the bank.

I regularly saw Jane on Sundays, at my grandparents' place. Dressed to the nines, she arrived dragging daughters and husband behind with the air of a weary devotee who hasn't got rid of the habit.

Jane-on-a-Sunday.

Winter or summer, she shows up with a tan. Her daughters plant themselves in front of the television; her husband rummages in the fringe with a scowl. At the table, her brother Harry takes a pinch of blonde tobacco out of the Export can, roles a length, and introduces it into a paper tube using a machine with a crank handle called a "stuffer."

Sunday is the day of roll-your-owns.

The visitors gather in the huge kitchen. The successive layers of linoleum make the floor spongy.

From the flattened cushions of her rocking chair, Jane's mother holds forth on the state of her goiter and the emphysema of Jane's father, who can be heard wheezing under the quilts. Black tea is drunk that has been sitting for hours on a burner. The latest news of the world gets discussed. They said on the radio that everything you are is inherited, *everything* bar nothing: research has proven it. Tony Bennett had a melanoma removed from his back. They said on the radio you should brush your tongue before going to bed, it's even more important than brushing your teeth. In Wyoming a woman gave birth to a baby with two heads. By caesarean, obviously.

Jane serves her daughters a snack. Jam cookies.

Harry has to have an operation on a disk in his back. He's practically sure he'll spend the rest of his life with a crooked spine and will have to creep along on a cane. He says that in a sheepish voice, his eyes fixed on the breasts of his sister Jane.

Jane asks him how he's getting along with his apartment hunt. "Forty-one years," she adds, "it's a little old to be living with Mama." Harry says it's not his fault. Because of his back, he hasn't got any choice.

Her mother, pouring steaming black tea, says she heard a good one. Says you'll never guess, then makes her audience languish a little, plumping up a cushion. Ears are pricked up. She opens her mouth. The sister-in-law of her brother Gordon has nose cancer. That's it. That's all.

I can't talk about Jane and me without mentioning the gondola *Mathilda*.

The gondola *Mathilda* belongs to the Roys. It's a large motorized floating platform, surrounded by a railing with pale canvas battening. The fabric has a desert island motif with a blonde; she's leaning against a palm tree and raising her arms to show off her pink breasts. The craft is fit out with bar stools, foam mattresses and camp coolers. A crossed chain of Chinese lanterns joins the gondola's four corners.

Weekdays, the *Mathilda* stays at anchor, but Saturday night, they get her ready for special excursions.

Jane's Saturday nights are spent aboard the gondola *Mathilda*.

The people on these special "cruises," for the most part couples recruited in nudist colonies, supply the beer and mosquito repellent. A babysitter is found for the children and the little craft is loaded. When the gondola leaves the dock, monsieur Roy, the slightly inebriated cruise director, strikes up the Caribbean song "Mathilda." Everybody loves that.

And the *Mathilda* drifts aimlessly on Little Lake Magog. Joyously disturbing the peace. You can hear people laughing. People shouting in unison. Once in a while, a naked man dives into the dark water on a dare or to fish out a bra that has been tossed overboard.

You can see the yellow-lit canvas of the *Mathilda's* awnings in the middle of the lake. Swarms of moths swirl around the lanterns. The boats of the curious float near. Sometimes they get invited aboard; sometimes they get sent away.

Excited, Jane puts on her make-up, emphasizes her cheekbones with rouge, thickens her eyelashes with black, retraces a chocolate line around her plum lips. Then she slips on a gum-pink string bikini, a Chinese peignoir and golden sandals. Still standing in front of the full-length mirror, she brushes her long black hair freshly conditioned with a hot oil treatment.

She performs all these acts while sucking a fresh cube of beef.

Her husband, Constable Michel Soucy— a veteran of the *Mathilda's* cruises— has slipped on a sky blue polo and khaki bermudas, with nothing under. He pats his cheeks with a sweet, greenish eau-de-toilette. He supplies a small case of cold Laurentide ale. A case of twelve. Nothing more.

Jane Soucy's Saturdays. The excitement of getting ready. The triumphant pushing off. The joyous cries at the heart of 1974.

Johanne Chouinard is the girl who comes to look after the daughters.

§

It was there, at Jane's, on Little Lake Magog, that I unpacked my duffel bag on July 1, 1974. I put my clothes away in the dresser, something no guy my age is used to doing. Puberty had just hit. I was moody and hating everything seemed to be the best way to keep face when confronted with a new situation.

While I waited for my aunt, I checked out her bookcases. She had *Dévoilements*, a popular black-covered coffee-table book illustrated with gigantic drawings from the cliffs of Peru; if you could believe the cut lines, what primitive people called God was nothing more or less than an extraterrestrial vessel. Leafing through, there was the picture of a rounded cross-section of an apple whose resemblance to the female sex was pointed out; this *proof* urged us to read the Old Testament in a new light.

With its back to the sofa, creating a sort of partition between the living room and the dining room, was a modern piano. My mind was made up: modern pianos had no class, were pretty little pieces of furniture that cost a lot of money for nothing.

Near the hearth, to start the fire, there was dry kindling and a pile of tabloids abundantly illustrated with gangsters full of bullet holes alternating with curvy blondes with open legs. The juxtaposition troubled me.

— Do you know how to swim at least? asked my aunt, who was giving me the once-over.

She smoked, holding the ashtray in her hand. She told me it would be too bad to spend a summer beside a swimming pool without knowing how to swim; it wasn't healthy at my age to be inside all the time. She herself did not know how to swim, had never been able to move in the water. I was a different case: I was young.

I told her her piano was lousy. She said it was the only one there was. She asked me if I knew how to play "Ebb Tide." I said no.

I sulked a little. I messed up everything I touched. I'd have rather stayed home, and spend the summer in my bedroom in Longueuil like I always did. My mother, under the impression that Magog would be good for me, had entrusted me to her sister Jane.

§

I have good memories of breakfasts with Jane. I am fifteen and I am alone with her. It's morning and she butters my toast. Her daughters are playing with their English friends on the beach. I get up late, like Jane. We have breakfast. It takes me forever to wake up. With puffy eyes, I stare at things. My gaze wanders back and forth between the glassy lake and my aunt's breasts, her perfect breasts in pink baby-doll pyjamas. In my head floats the image of a goldfish tossed about peacefully in its bag of water.

I tell her again that her piano's out of tune. Not in the least put out, she repeats it's the only one there is.

— Do you know how to play "Love Story"? she asks, a sudden gleam in her eye.

I tell her again it's not my kind of thing. I don't play anything later than Dvorak. She never heard of him.

The Chouinard girl is coming to babysit Saturday night. Jane says she and my uncle have a party to go to on the gondola. It's an adult party, so I am not invited. The Chouinard kid is my age, she remarks, amused.

§

My uncle, Constable Soucy, and I, keep our distance. We've nothing to say to each other. When I'm around, he gets inarticulate, and that makes him furious. He's a ruddy guy, kind of beefy; even when relaxed, his face is red as if he's just been bending over. These days, he talks only about his knee, and he can't help noticing I'm not interested in hearing about his knee. He fell on it coming out of McDonald's, and, if he plays his cards right, the court case he's launched against them might assure him a very comfortable early retirement. He's sure he'll win.

I have no comment.

He's the one who brings the sexy tabloids home from work. If I've understand correctly, the police get them for nothing. He piles them by the fireplace.

Nights when the moon is bright, I sleep badly. I get up and leaf through the tabloids in the living room, close to the plate-glass window, reading in the light from the sky. The pictures are grey and yellow. The puddles of blood look black near the fat faces of the Mafiosi. The behinds of the girls are as pale as sea shells.

§

Saturday night rolls around. The Chouinard girl's not interested in guys my age and she doesn't mind telling me. She's already gone out with a man who has a car and it's no secret.

She settles down in front of the TV. They're showing a low budget film where wolves attack village people at night. I leaf through an illustrated encyclopaedia with my young cousin.

Jane-on-a-Saturday-night.

In the corner of my eye, I can see the *Mathilda* floating beyond the living room picture window, like a yellow flower on the contaminated water.

§

Hanon's finger exercises are repetitive. They are meant for warming up your fingers and it's with a sigh that I set to it.

— That's really boring! comments Jane.

Her frankness amuses me.

Jane laughs, coughing.

Jane has always had a deep cough. She calls it "hereditary emphysema." She does her clapping every day. My uncle often helps. She spits. Sometimes she cries out while coughing stuff up. Sometimes my uncle hits her too hard and makes a bruise on her back. It's part of the routine. Nobody mentions it.

When I was little, my mother said that her big sister Jane was not long for this world because she had refused, out of vanity, to put on her boots in winter when she was fifteen. Having been nurtured on this myth, my Aunt Jane seemed to me the most beautiful and the most elegant. The most impressive, too: she would not live very long.

§

The Moon is a half-moon. When night falls, the light has a peculiar effect on the greasy soup called a lake.

My visit to my Aunt Jane's is counted out in Saturdays.

She brushes her long black hair while sucking a strip of sirloin. My uncle counts out his beer and sniffs under his arms. Young Johanne Chouinard will arrive shortly to make supper for the girls.

The *Mathilda* is all decked out.

Jane is in a hurry. The waning Moon will make the men crazy. She can feel it. She sucks her beef to get out all the blood. It tastes of life.

I don't trust young Johanne Chouinard; she gets on my nerves when she's around. Saturday evenings, I leave her with my cousins in front of the TV and I go out for a walk, alone on the lakeside road. A long walk.

I hear shouts coming from the *Mathilda*. I prick up my ears. I am spying on them. I try to make out what they are saying, who's saying what words emanating from the middle of the lake. My heart races thinking what's going on there, and I am at a loss because I can't really picture it.

I sit on the ground, on the road, and without knowing why, I sob, hiding my face.

I finally feel better and I manage to look at the *Mathilda* more calmly.

The gondola looks completely adrift. As if no one is steering it. Is that possible?

§

Johanne Chouinard is an obnoxious little brat. It's because of her that everything falls apart a few days later, a day when my uncle got an unexpected day off, when my aunt was supposed to be having coffee at the neighbour's, when my cousins were supposed to be taking a hike with the Doucets and when yours truly was supposed to be pounding away on the piano.

I heard everything.

Jane was furious. Down in the basement, she ran bang into the young Chouinard coming out of the furnace room with my uncle behind doing up his fly. The girl's knees were black with soot and she was shamelessly wiping off her swollen lips, using her arm. In a calm voice, Constable Soucy accused my aunt of lacking an open mind.

Jane climbed up the stairs crying tears of rage, her hand over her mouth to keep down her disgust. There were marks on her arms. While he was giving her a talking to, my uncle'd held her wrists in a vice grip.

At the living room window, she cooled her face on the pane. Her husband's car took off in a cloud of dust.

Jane's eyes were swollen. She wiped her nose with ball of Kleenex bunched up in her hand. Without turning her head, she asked me to play Chopin's "Polonaise." I told her it was too difficult for someone at my level.

— It's because of my piano... you don't like my piano... she said, wiping her eyes.

She poured herself a Scotch and lit a long cigarette. I picked out "London Bridge"... using two fingers to fill up the silence.

I finally asked her why she was crying. She said her life was a tragedy. She had never learned how to drive a car. Once, she had tried. My uncle had let her take over the wheel to see if she could, and in less than a second she'd driven into a ditch by a field. The barbed wire had scratched the hood. Her daughters screamed hysterically in the back seat. My uncle's face grew white.

We laughed. Jane kept crying through her smile.

I started a Bach prelude, the prelude in C. Played slowly, it's easy not to make mistakes. Jane closed her eyes and let herself drift away on the arpeggios. She didn't talk.

She was scaring me.

That night, from my bed, I could see Jane, from the back, in her window. She was dancing in full view. Her body loose. Caressing herself, rocking back and forth. She was swallowing, in little sips, an amber Rusty Nail which, shot through with the light from the anti-bug bulb on the veranda, looked almost orange, and she was lost in her thoughts. She leaned against the window, leaving the trace of her fists on the pane.

All night long. Limper and limper.

She would taste her Drambuie, then go back to the rocking she was consoling herself with. She caressed her breasts. Floating. She was in another world, like a woman at prayer.

Jane-it's-Sunday.

On the radio, they said milk could cause cancer. A woman from New Mexico has given birth to a little girl without ever having conceived. To the utter astonishment of the obstetricians, she was still a virgin when she gave birth. It's because of the hormones they put in the meat. Carol Burnett is seeing a psychiatrist.

Jane listens to the latest news while preparing a plate of jam cookies for her daughters, who are playing with their Barbies in the living room.

Harry is busy with his roll-your-owns. He can't stop sneezing: he has developed an allergy to raw tobacco: it doesn't mean he can't still smoke. Harry's hands move slowly; it's not his fault: the painkillers that he takes for his back are too strong.

Jane looks tired. That's what her mother says, pouring her some thick tea.

— I went to bed late last night, Jane offers in explanation.

Harry, teasing, says his sister Jane, at forty-seven, needs her "beauty sleep." He tells her that, looking at her breasts.

The tea is bitter. It has been on the stove too long.

My aunt's room costs a lot of money. It's a private room. The ceiling is high and the walls are a kind of dull pinky brown. It's a good thing some kids have come and pasted a cut-out toothless jack o'lantern and the drawing of a witch on a broom on the window. It's Hallowe'en tonight. You can hear the laughter of children at the end of the corridor.

Outside, in the park, one or two leaves hang from the trees. On the ground, everything is rust-coloured.

The air around my aunt bristles with tension. She says that this year, for Hallowe'en, she's dressed up in terminal phase. My mother and I laugh along with her.

She sits up straight in her bed. A perforated tube runs under her nose, and up over her ears like a pair of glasses. Another tube, with one end in a bottle of solution is stuck into her arm. She takes only liquid chocolate meals sipped through a straw.

She gripes about the hospital. Some nurses don't even know how to stick in a needle without tearing a vein. She shows her bruised arms and says, "Look what they've done to me."

My mother looks sorry.

Without being obvious, I avert my gaze: anything that has to do with a needle sticking into skin makes me feel sick to look at.

My mother is worried. She describes her symptoms: at the age of fifty-two she has been bleeding for seventeen days. She feels her strength draining away hour by hour. Her big sister Jane says, "In our family we bleed long. Remember, Helen had her period..." (and, without missing a beat, she looks me in the eye and mutters "You don't like me" and continues her conversation)... "Helen had her period for something like forty days. They made her drink steak juice... Have you tried steak juice?"

While my mother details her food intake, item by item, I sit on my straight chair and wonder why Jane said that to me. I'd just in fact been thinking that the morphine was giving her second sight: she could, with one well-aimed comment, bluntly reveal some visitor's darkest thoughts. In the last few days, any relative displaying forced cheerfulness was quickly put in his place. She sees everything, sees through everything.

I take the opportunity of her glancing in my direction to say in a low voice, "You're wrong, Auntie. It isn't true." She indicates with a shrug I should forget it. Nothing matters to her.

She says this hospital has forced her to give up raw steak,

sex and cigarettes. "All the good things." She has also given up on the possibility of a heart-lung transplant. At her age (sixty-five) and in her state, they'd made it clear it wasn't likely. Any donor organ would automatically go to a younger, healthier woman.

Even dying, Jane still has some of her beauty, some of her elegance, some of her rage.

Her doctor won't give her a fatal injection. He won't discuss it. No matter how hard she pleads, he insists it's immoral, and the word makes her see red. It's war between them.

In the meantime, she watches reruns of *The Golden Girls* and, as soon as the nurse walks out of the room, she nibbles on the raw hamburger her husband slips to her. In her purse, in case she gets an urge to break the rules, is a cigarette rolled up in a Kleenex. It's nice to know the cigarette is there.

Visiting time is over. My mother jingles her car keys and asks me if I want a lift. She promises her sister she will come by tomorrow.

In the hospital corridor, toddlers in black-Dracula or devil-red costumes hug their candy bags and run as fast as they can to make their capes fly out. Little girls in tutus are Star Fairies or pure white Princesses.

My mother, with her keys in her hand, waits in the doorway. She discreetly wipes her eyes as I kiss Jane goodbye.

Jane squeezes me tight and thanks me for coming. She holds me in her arms a minute. We don't move. We don't speak.

Gradually, I am flooded with her pain, feel the depth of her suffering. She is old and feeble. It weighs down my chest. It weighs on me. I can feel the lead weight of her ancestors who live within her heart like Russian dolls. They are dark beings, buried in darkness. They suck me in. They suck in my breath. I can feel my breath being taken away from me. I breathe less. I stop breathing.

I feel like vomiting.

I stiffen and, instinctively, I back off.

I am embarrassed by my reaction. I don't know what made me do it.

Jane puts her hand on my cheek and smiles compassionately. "You see," she says in a low voice, "I'm right. You don't like me."

1994

JAVEX

Marie-Johanne Beaudin pays for her subscription. The pharmacist has given her metronidazole capsules, which, with their pale green and pale grey ends make the most beautifully coloured hodgepodge in their bottle. In a voice loud enough so the people standing in line behind her will hear, she asks if German Shepherds can take them. Shocked, the pharmacist shakes his head, but it is clear he has no idea. Marie-Johanne heaves a sigh and, with a curt gesture, picks up her bag.

Marie-Johanne looks Scandinavian with her pale blonde hair, her blue eyes and her rosy cheeks. Her full lips (Gauguin lips, she calls them) give her a sulky look. She's wearing a sky blue overall that makes her behind look bigger and a white blouse with puffy sleeves. A round don't-mess-with-me looking woman, she doesn't make eye contact when walking down the street.

She's on her way to the Vocational School; she always goes there on foot. That's where she works. It's just around the corner.

As she walks, she throws back a green and grey pill with a swallow of mineral water. Her underwear is sticky; the greenish discharge gives off a foul smell. An unpleasant symptom. At the clinic, the eyes of a young doctor with a propensity for didactics lit up as he spelled out how the trichomonas had to be blasted from her insides. She cut him off before the end of his lecture, told him she wasn't retarded, and he could address her as a normal person. Now that she's alone, she laughs, thinking of little antibiotic pills as ballistics.

At the Vocational School, Marie-Johanne Beaudin empties the dryers and folds the towels. When the piles are standing straight and perfect, she rolls her laundry cart over to her supply-attendant's wicket.

Sometimes, when she's sure no one's around, she buries her face in the towel nap, breathing in the detergent odour. Breathing it in deeply.

The student hairdressers arrive for the evening courses around six o'clock. The girls go to Marie-Johanne to get their dummy head, towels, basket of curlers, bottles of dye, peroxide, shampoo. It is Marie-Johanne who sees they are supplied. Her wicket is in the basement, at the end of the main corridor; people call it "the shed." I'm going to the shed... Bring me back a towel from the shed...

The shed girl...

Traffic is heavy before and after classes. During, it's quiet; the shed girl reads Lautréamont, and sighs, finding him old-fashioned. Or else she reads Bataille; she could do better with her eyes closed. She reads Duras; Duras is simple to the point of lazy.

In the shed, beside a pile of white towels, the attendant sighs loudly as she reads. With her chin squished up by her fist, she looks like she's sulking.

Before closing shop, Marie-Johanne drags the laundry bags of dirty towels to the laundry room where they will be bleached.

Anointing the laundry room air.

In the evening class, there's a student hairdresser whose name, like hers, is Marie-Johanne, Marie-Johanne Daunais. She's from Mascouche. She is living with her aunt while she completes her hairdressing course in Montréal. A tubby, eternally cheerful girl, the fold of her wrist is drawn as tightly around as string on a piece of white sausage.

The towel attendant has noticed her, because of their common name, but also because she sees in the simple girl a kind of raw purity. She calls her (which makes her quietly die laughing) "Little Miss Goodfellow."

"Little Miss Goodfellow" is allowed to slide up the wicket and go in and chew the fat with the "laundry shed girl" who has made up her mind that such a privilege could "up" the kid's popularity rating a notch or two in the eyes of her classmates.

They talk about everything and nothing. They kill time.

Pretending to straighten a pile of towels, Marie-Johanne enlightens the kid on what beautiful breasts she has, despite her baby fat. As she says so, she quickly turns and feels up the bouncy breasts. "Really beautiful!" she insists, hands all over the kid's chest. The kid, her cheeks on fire, tears out of the shed yelling *Help*.

Marie-Johanne heaves a bored sigh. The young Mascouchoise is stupid. She has spoiled everything.

She has nothing to do, so the towel girl opens her book again. An essay on the aesthetics of Burne-Jones, made easy.

At eleven, Marie-Johanne goes home. She has a room over La Patate à Gérard, a twenty-four-hour snack bar. It was the place's name that grabbed her. She always says, with a poker face, she's nesting "on top of Gérard's potatoes" and it feels pretty good. She's been there for ten years. She likes it.

The narrow corridor leading to the door of her room is greasy. The hallway's walls, thickly plastered and painted pale green, are lit by a grey leaded glass early-twentieth oeil-de-boeuf; here and there, the yellow linoleum sticks to the soles of your shoes.

The room seems big enough to provide for the basics. There's a mountain of books on the work table (no room to eat). There are two doors: one opening into the tiny bathroom; another, onto a tiny fire-escape platform. The window of that door is almost opaque. It boasts a greyness made of cement dust, city grime, and the French-fry grease floating up from Gerard's. You can vaguely make out the yellow halo of an anti-bug bulb on the fire-escape platform.

Marie-Johanne undresses, tossing her clothes on the dresser. She puts on a very large grey t-shirt with a tomato sauce stain down the front. The skin on her thighs is lumpy and perfectly white.

Over the opened sofa bed, three dog posters are hung. Highly coloured images of dogs with touched-up teeth panting in the heat of the projectors. Animals, brushed, groomed, patiently poised on astro-turf.

Recently, Marie-Johanne has become a dog lover. An extremely passionate dog lover.

In the unmade bed, whimpering like he has to go, a German shepherd is licking off the pus stuck to his reddened penis. Though his flanks are a little scrawny, he's a solid, full-grown animal. She lets him go out on the balcony. He bounds over the green garbage bags and pisses on his little square of *Presse* newsprint.

Marie-Johanne refuses to give him a name. When necessary, she calls him "You." She thinks people who give dogs Christian names are stupid.

She swallows a metronidazole tablet. She needs to figure out how to give one to the dog. His nose is runny. And his discharge is soiling the carpeting.

Night has begun. Under a violent college lamp, Marie-Johanne writes in large round letters, in handwriting that shows a lot of character according to the graphology manuals she's read. She uses a German rapido she fills with pale brown ink. The pen cost something. She bought it ten years ago when she was thinking of going to art school.

She's working on the back of various sheets of recycled paper: old university papers, Trade School forms, photocopies of her breast, her hands or her bottom that she snuck into the school principal's office to make: she was thinking of papering the walls of her bathroom with them.

She writes a paragraph of her thesis.

Certainly, irony is a possible means of surviving scandal, for distance protects. But can one be saved from ellipsis? There is Verfremdungseffekt and Verfremdungseffekt!

Marie-Johanne compliments herself on her turn of phrase. Every day she sits down and writes a line or two; in a year, the thesis will be completed. Each line is definitive. Nothing will be revised. Period.

Her paragraph finished, she doodles art-nouveau ornaments around her thesis title. Her hand is precise. Talented. She scribbles, head bent, as if she were talking on the telephone.

Her thesis title— *The Pornographer Ellipsis*— is an oxymoron that she dreamed up to titillate her thesis director. When she thinks of the prof's rapturizing, she kills herself laughing. She's not moved by his praise. She despises him: he is a tall, thin, bald man and if he were *truly* intelligent, he would call her on it. If he were *truly* intelligent, he would see through Marie-Johanne Beaudin's irony.

She pulls on a pair of baggy jeans and a plaid shirt. She goes down to the snack bar on the ground floor. The neon lights are garish. A cheerful homeless guy gives her a low bow as she enters. She ignores him. She indicates she wants the usual, and they make her three steamy hot dogs with mustard and cabbage, lots of mustard. To go. In a little brown stapled bag.

Back in her room, she wolfs down her supper in the green light of the television.

Marie-Johanne likes the way the excess yellow mustard looks slathered over the wiener, running out at the ends. It's an appearance of plenty. She eats alone, a napkin on her lap. She closes her eyes when she bites into the soft bread.

She lets the dog in, who climbs up on the sofa bed and snuggles down against a pillow. Under the frozen smile of Lassie.

Marie-Johanne opens his gullet and sticks a metronidazole capsule down his throat. She immediately claps her hands, right above his nose. The dog, startled, swallows the capsule.

She looks at her dog. Her dog's brown eyes. His standing-up ears. In her opinion, animals are *essentially* hairy. That's the right word. Their very *essence* is hair.

Kneeling in front of the toilet bowl, Marie-Johanne sticks her fingers in her mouth and vomits up the equivalent of one-and-a-half hot dogs. She's proud of this regurgitation technique. She invented it herself. It allows her to eat her fill without getting fat.

She throws back a large glass of Pepsi to rinse out her mouth.

On TV, the channel twelve late-night program, Louise-Josée Mondoux† is talking about the Camping Fair at the Olympic Stadium. She articulates every word perfectly. Her hair is platinum. She's impeccable. In her nice pink suit.

On her bed, hands clasped behind her head, Marie-Johanne stares at Louise-Josée Mondoux, whose name she's always liked because it sounds like a promise. Watching Louise-Josée in front of a shiny army of trailers turns her on. She moves her hand down to her pubis and grabs her triangle of pubic hair, bearing down as if to tightly close her outer lips. She squeezes. It tightens. She crosses her legs and strains. She holds back.

The dog right beside her whimpers; a sound that approaches disquiet.

Marie-Johanne thinks about trailers and her gaze grows blank. Empty.

---

† Mondoux— literally, my sweet one

The trailer.

The Beaudins' trailer.

The Beaudins, the boudins.‡

They were only supposed to live there for three months. It was longer. Two years, Marie-Johanne recalls.

In Longueuil, a nice neat suburb, because of their mother's carelessness, the Beaudins' bungalow had burned down. In the middle of the straight row of little houses of white Spanish-style stucco, of red brick and rustic-style stones, stood a black pile, broken glass, rivers of soot. The Beaudins' lawn was filthy.

After four, during that free floating hour between school's out and dinner-time, children headed for the front lawn of the soiled home to breathe in the smell of adventure. The vinyl stretched across windows smashed by firemen with their axes and the boards nailed over the door inspired reruns of rescue operations. After school until supper time, they hovered, dumb in face of disaster, hardly believing their eyes, at a loss for words before this shattering extraordinary event, that was something to talk about.

‡ literally, blood sausages

In the course of time, the stinky smell of the black house dissipated, and, by virtue of piecemeal renovations done with makeshift materials, the house finally stood back up in line.

For the time it took to be cured of her depression, Marie-Johanne's mother was institutionalized. And for the time the repairs to the house would take, monsieur Beaudin had settled his daughters— his four "blondes"— in a huge trailer planted in the yard behind the black bungalow. It was only supposed to be for three months. The time it would take for repairs.

It was all supposed to be temporary.

At the high school, Marie-Johanne kept her cool as they jeered at her. "Beaudins, boudins." But she was not ashamed of the family trailer. She was not ashamed *exactly*. She could clearly see the irony of the situation. It was perfectly clear to her. Ultimately, to camp behind one's house was to kill yourself laughing. She faced her classmates in Secondary 1, her head high, smiling to herself.

She turned up in class with black kohl around her eyes (which really stood out against her milk-white skin) and no one made the connection with her sooty house. Her joke fell flat.

In the final analysis, the kids who laughed at the Beaudin girls were simpleminded types who took everything at "face value"; and those who didn't laugh were even worse.

At first, the trailer was liveable. It was special, an unexpected holiday. The Beaudin girls were having a totally good time pretending to be gypsies. At night, giggling in their sleeping bags, they had trouble getting to sleep.

They'd be back in the house soon. For sure.

Taking a shower was a Saturday event that lasted all day, given how long it took for the hot water tank to fill up. During the week, the Beaudin girls washed themselves in the sink after they finished doing the supper dishes. Because the drain was slow, they often emptied the pan of greasy water in the yard. Then, naturally, though there was no rule about it, they waited until their father was asleep before undressing to wash.

It wasn't supposed to be for long.

The winter months were hard. With sticky tape, they'd insulated everything: windows, corners, door. They lived in a damp bubble.

In this hermetically sealed den, the father, monsieur Beaudin, a short round man, perspired abundantly. Marie-Johanne remembers the washcloth he used to leave, screwed up in a ball, on the edge of the kitchen sink. She remembers a short man with a round stomach who always left curly hair in the shower, black hair stuck in the Ivory soap bar.

It wasn't supposed to be for long.

Monsieur Beaudin had the wheeze of a fat man. At night, his bronchial breathing filled the damp trailer. The morbid sound penetrated everything. He was everywhere, and his hair stayed stuck to the mildew of the shower curtain.

Marie-Johanne curls down under the sheets. She is thinking about the perfect platinum curls of Louise-Josée. Her stomach growls. She feels a little hungry. It tightens. A sign she's losing weight.

Marie-Johanne falls asleep happy.

Around noon, shortly after she wakens, Marie-Johanne gets a phone-call from the Vocational School principal. She must report directly to his office when she gets in. In a piqued tone of voice, she answers "Okay, okay" and hangs up on him.

She knows what's up. The Vocational School principal, monsieur Beaudin, her father, will give her a lecture about teasing "Little Miss Goodfellow." Marie-Johanne will say she's sorry. She'll keep her head bowed, to make it look more convincing, and things will be back to normal.

It's not the first time this has happened. Papa will adopt his stern voice and say it's outrageous that a talented girl like Marie-Johanne has never amounted to anything. Marie-Johanne has completed her doctoral courses. Marie-Johanne is thirty-four years old, soon thirty-five. Marie-Johanne could have done anything she wanted with the education he paid for. Instead of that, she persists in embarrassing him in his own school.

With her head lowered, Marie-Johanne will promise not to do it again and life will go on.

At school, the frail receptionist says kindly, "Oh, Mademoiselle Beaudin! Your father wants to see you right away." Marie-Johanne keeps on her pouty face, ignoring her.

She knocks on her father's door. Three sharp knocks.

He tells her to come in.

Without waiting for her to take a seat, he says, "Go to the shed and get your things."

Marie-Johanne looks at him, right in the eye; she doesn't understand.

Her father makes himself clear. During her nine years as laundry attendant, Marie-Johanne has received three complaints of harassing women hairdressers. The young Marie-Johanne Daunais is the last straw. "Leave," he finishes.

Marie-Johanne's throat wobbles a little.

—You can't do that... What am I going to do? she asks.

—The paperwork's already done. Go.

Marie-Johanne snivels. She apologizes; she promises not to do it again; she promises to do her best. She folds her hands.

Her father stares at the ceiling, impatiently.

Marie-Johanne approaches him and begs.

With his hands behind his back, monsieur Beaudin turns towards the large window that looks out on downtown. He is waiting for his daughter to leave so he can get back to work.

In the basement corridor where the hairdressers are bustling about, people gape at Marie-Johanne dragging herself along. Like she has two heads, each noisily blowing its nose.

In the shed, somewhere on the orders shelf are books belonging to her. Gombrowicz. Sade. Villemaire. With a lethargic gesture, she picks them up, then, as if suddenly exhausted, lets everything fall to the ground.

She runs her hand over a pile of towels, all white and spongy. She squeezes them to feel their softness. They are pure white clouds in the sky of a fairy tale. Untouched clouds. She puts the corner of the towel back in place, to make it perfectly square.

She buries her face in the white nub. The little threads tickle her cheek. She breathes in the odour of Javex. It's a camphorous odour that fills up the throat, kills the dirt, cleans the insides, opens the respiratory passages and settles in the heart with phosphorescent violence. Her shoulders are shaking with sobs; Marie-Johanne can no longer stop crying. She hiccups, with her face nuzzled in the white pile.

She lowers her face and kisses the pile of towels at its base. She rubs her face against them like cats do when they want to leave their odour on their masters' calves.

When she calms down and her breathing gets back to normal, Marie-Johanne is exhausted. Her eyes are dull. Their whites are red, her lips are wet, and she is talking to herself out loud, like a homeless woman, without taking notice of the hairdressers who are helping themselves to towels in the laundry shed.

"I will not survive... I will not survive..."

1994

SHADES OF GRAY

Ruthie Hooppell, the good ship *Benedict*, Welsh rigour... A difficult tale to weave. A story I must try over again using things nobody knows but me. People will still say I am making it up. That I am mistaken.

I know she makes porridge. Each morning, Ruthie takes the porridge off the burner and stirs a spoon of salted cream into it. It has a beige gray consistency. Her husband comes up behind her, places a hot hand on her corset and kisses her on the neck. She automatically pushes him away.

They've been doing this for twenty years. It's normal.

Ruthie doesn't love her husband.

When she got off the boat in Verdun at the end of the century, she chose this Liverpool Englishman, a little vague, and too tall. He was a nice man, thoughtful. She chose him to found a solid household, to be responsible, and above all, to be sure to never forget Paul Dubois, a French-Canadian, strong as a bull, who loved life and had a perpetual hard-on.

Paul Dubois had seduced her. They'd seen each other three times. She was fourteen years old, had pale skin, and couldn't utter a word of French; he misused a few English words, laughing at his faults. When he wasn't around, she paced up and down the alley, and when he showed up to see her, she felt troubled. There was no question of her giving herself to him (her mother would have cut her throat), but she let him feel her up, protesting a little, for the sake of appearances; he grabbed her around the waist and rubbed his hips against her thigh so she could feel the hard lump in his pants; he held her close to him, in his strong arms, so his heat could be felt across her stiff corset. She didn't understand a single word of what he was saying, but it was obvious he was constantly referring to "it." Such an "earthy" man couldn't be talking about anything else.

On the *Benedict*, Mary, Ruthie's mother, had passed the better part of the crossing begging her offspring to remain nice girls. My daughters, she declared, we didn't leave that filthy mining town to come and hobnob with the peasants. When Mary spoke of the miners of Cardiff— which, after a glass of wine for medicinal purposes, she called Caerdydd— she didn't conceal her disgust, warming to her tale like a storyteller. The green valleys were mined with dangerous fox holes and her father, Andrew Gwyn, was a black animal who only emerged from his hole to copulate, a primitive creature, a beast who couldn't distinguish his wife from his daughters. In opting for the New World, Mary was hoping for better for her girls. She was aiming higher.

The parables of lost girls that burdened Ruthie's puberty had been enough to make her renounce the evil consequences of stolen pleasures. She'd made the right choice by marrying the tall English guy from Liverpool. A reticent man who never had a thing to say about anything. He kissed her on the neck; she automatically pushed him away. That was it, the way things were, for Ruthie Hooppell.

Ruthie sets the bowls of porridge on the table. Each child is allowed two ladles full. Armed with a knife, her son Gordon hacks at the hardened brown sugar in the bottom of the jar. Her three daughters daydream and look out the window; the hardest thing in the world is for them to wake up. The eldest is thinking about her secret love, a hefty French-Canadian, who can hold his booze. With the exception of Gordon's lapping, the Hooppells breakfast in silence.

While they sit at the table wolfing down their mush behind her back, Ruthie eats a yellow apple, sitting on her bench, facing the wall. She's waiting for them to go, the whole lot. The men to the railway yard, the women to the factory. After which, she will be able to devote her day to washing and tidying.

But the eldest girl needs a talking to. The eldest is lovesick. You can tell. This has got to be nipped in the bud; it will be.

Gordon and his father get up and jam on their railway workers' caps. The girls get up in turn. They work in a pickling factory. They put gherkins in jars.

The eldest is thinking about her lover. Fitful as moodiness, her secret either weighs her down or raises her spirits. Ruthie has often lectured her. *If it feels good, then it is not good for you.*★ A rigid morality, square, uptight, as heavy as a bucket of coal, dragged over here from the old country... If Ruthie knew what her eldest was doing with her boyfriend behind the grassy knoll... A Catholic, on top of everything else...

As soon as the eldest daughter has finished clearing the table, Ruthie calls her over.

They are alone in the kitchen.

Averting her gaze, Ruthie says that pleasure opens the door to pain. She should know that since the beginning of time, nobody ever had one without the other. It's the law of hard knocks, but a fair law. Only doing one's duty leads to a peaceful life. It was the case for her, it is the case on this day in 1929, and it will be the case later, for her girls.

The eldest daughter asks her mother why she's saying that. Ruthie briskly turns and stings her cheek with a firm slap. The eldest is crying. Ruthie stands straight, her arms crossed. Her eldest has got the message.

— *Have you forgotten my motto?*★

The eldest sobs.

— *Say it,*★ Ruthie orders.

— *If it feels good, then it's not good for me.*★

On that note, Ruthie dismisses her in a firm voice, saying that one day, she will thank her.

Ruthie Hooppell. Hers is a story of failure. You might say of repressed passages.

The only real memory I have of Ruthie Hooppell, my maternal great-grandmother, is the image of an old woman with a round face and swollen eyes, sitting on the lawn swing in Farnham. Under an enormous pine. In 1965. Not more than two years before she died. It's summer. The countryside is beautiful. It's hot. When the cicada sings, we can't hear ourselves think. My grandmother's house is situated on top of a hill, with a magnificent view of the beige field and the leafy forest. I am six years old.

Granny Hooppell impresses me because she knows how to speak Gaelic; they say a few words of it slip out when she gets mad. Even if I am young, I know not many people speak this language. She is visiting her eldest daughter (my grandmother) who is going all out to please her and, like a maid who's been allowed into the living room for tea-time and would give anything to go back to her dusting, Great-grandma's smiling non-stop, at everyone, without saying a word. Her smile exposes her toothless gums. My brother says she has an Eskimo smile and that earns him a cuff on the back of the head.

Sitting in the lawn swing under the large pine, Granny Hooppell has gone off by herself to eat a yellow apple that she peels with a knife, an apple she picked up off the ground under the apple tree by the driveway, a wormy apple nobody would have wanted, a yellow apple, ripe and soft, that she is going to munch on with her tongue and her gums.

I remember how swollen her feet were. There are brown spots on her taut skin.

I am six years old. I go to join her on the swing, and ask her, in my perfect English, if it's true that she saw it rain grasshoppers when she was little. All she does is smile. I ask her if there were as many as people say; I come up with astronomical figures. She laughs and ventures one sentence, only one. She says that the men made fires outside to fill the sky with smoke, and as for the women, they stayed in and the windows were black and you couldn't see the sun any more. That's all. I want shocking specifics but she contents herself with a smile, munching her yellow apple. I end up telling the story myself, stopping for approval of every detail.

When all is said and done, I am disappointed. She hardly talks to me. She eats her apple with the knife, piling the spotted yellow peels in her apron.

It is because I am around that she keeps her mouth shut. I noticed that. When she is talking to her daughter, all I have

to do is draw near or happen to walk by for her to stop talking. My father says it's nothing to worry about. She's like that
because we speak French.

1995

CLAN

The Laporte and Sons Funeral Home is typical of the South Shore. It is surrounded by an empty field and looks out on the auto route. Only the façade has been bricked and decorated; the sides are covered with aluminum imitation-wood planks, as if nobody ever saw them.

Going back to the South Shore is always trying.

I breakfasted on a coffee with cream and a croissant with butter; I have heartburn. The cold air feels like a good bath. It's a windy spring morning. A wind that comes from distant empty stretches and is chilled by the dirty snow along the roadsides. It is the first day of the year when you can go without boots.

We are burying my grandfather. Eighty-three years old. Four children. Half a dozen horses. Arthritis. Glaucoma. Emphysema. I'm probably forgetting a few.

I hadn't seen my grandmother since her daughter Jane's funeral, four years ago. She arrives on the arm of her sister Helen. She doesn't cry well. She opens her mouth wide as if she had a cramp in her stomach. But no sighs, no wails come out, nothing. Like someone cut the sound. This display is getting on my nerves. Maybe it's her lack of elegance: that's no way to cry in front of other people.

My Aunt Suzy doesn't try to hide it: she doesn't like mourning. She's wearing a dress of bright red lace, layered with fringed panels and worn with cherry-red fishnet stockings and matching shoes. She stays behind in the parking lot to smoke a cigarette. With the back-lighting of the cement intersection in the distance, she looks naked and proud of it. My Great Aunt Helen, who has come especially from Hamilton, bursts out laughing when she sees her.

These are my people.

I didn't have much of a relationship with my grandfather. The odd memory, his prickly cheek that my mother made me kiss. Otherwise, he avoided eye contact; he had nothing to say to me. He spoke to me only once: about an enraged grass-snake.

In those days he lived in the country. My brother and I were chasing snakes in the potato patch. My brother was good at grabbing them by the neck. The big striped black ones with yellow stomachs, the little brown ones with red stomachs and neck bands, the thin nervous bottle green ones. We used to pat them and hold them up within an inch of our noses, then let them go. The hunt took up entire afternoons. In my memory, my role appears to have been restricted to standing around and getting excited as my brother energetically flushed them out with a stick. Except one time. The grass snake was black and thick as an inner tube and, from the moment we saw it, figuring it was a pregnant female, therefore twice as aggressive, my brother had given up trying to catch it. All the same, we'd teased her, with quite a long branch, to make her squirm. In mid-flight, the snake, in a panic, turned on us. She coiled up in a mass and, with her head hoisted high, she opened her mouth; she was furious. Ready to defend myself, I picked up a stone as big as a billiard ball. To my great surprise, my brother ordered me to kill her. With his sanctioning, I held the stone at arm's length, moving close to the creature and staring her in the eyes. Like the angel who appeared to Abraham, my grandfather rushed up, casting aspersions on us. Out of breath, exasperated, he gave us what-for about how useful the grass snake is in the fields; it eats harmful bugs. While he sang its praises, the snake disappeared under the low leaves of the garden.

My brother and I stood there sheepishly. It seems to me it was the only time my grandfather spoke to me directly. Or else it is I who, for my own purposes, reduces our contacts to that. My sole legacy: Do not kill grass snakes.

In the plush room, the air is heavy with perfume. The deceased's coffin is flanked by two generous wreaths with ribbons bearing gold letters and a vase of daisies. In the family, people think it's a waste of money to buy flowers. The deceased is not in a position to appreciate them and you only end up throwing them out anyway. The flowers that are there were sent by an insurance company and by my Aunt Suzy's boss; the bouquet of daisies is courtesy of Laporte and Sons.

My Uncle Harry leads me to the cloakroom, where he hands me a Zellers bag full of gnarled scrapbooks and old yellowed newspapers. The bag smells strongly of horse. Before dying, my grandfather expressed the wish that I, the writer, should write a history of old Longueuil, giving the family a prominent place. A sort of municipal saga where our ancestors have the lead roles. To this end, to cut down on the research, he asked that I be given this bag stuffed with yellowed newspaper clippings; he kept it like a treasure in the barn cupboard, along with the castration scissors and cow ointment. There are entire scrapbooks of the *Courrier du Sud*. Articles on the blacksmiths from the nostalgia series *This happened... even in Longueuil!* A reproduction of early-century light-bulb ads. Clippings glued with white paste on a calendar of girls with pink nipples or in a blue spiral notebook, the same kind they made us buy in catechism class. Recipes for a disinfectant ointment. Death notices circled with a felt pen. An illustrated insert: *Are the Vikings our true ancestors?*

I take a seat, the yellowed bundles stuck between my feet. The odour rises, like the sweat of a palomino, like rivers of smoky piss wetting hay. I feel my shoulders sagging. The emanating odours become entangled with the whiffs of button carnations, and roses. Also with waves of formaline issuing, I presume, from the corpse.

My grandfather was a bored old man. His legacy is pathetic. I could leave the stinky bag in my mother's car. Discreetly. After all, he's her father, not mine.

My Aunt Suzy makes me laugh. A woman of the world, she chats while stroking her calf to smooth out her stocking (the candy red fishnet) under the gaze of a toothless old guy with rosy cheeks. She winks at me.

My mother comes over. She sits down next to me. She leans forward and looks serious. She is wondering if her father forgave her before he died. She whispers, keeps bringing her hand up to her mouth; she tells me that hardly anybody knows the bad thing she did. At the age of eight, she killed Chucker, her father's favourite horse. He already had two horses, but they were lame old things and soon got turned into meat. Chucker was different. He had character and he was a beauty. He had the hues of a Siamese cat: a sandy coat with coal black mane, tale and feet. He was tall, thin and, you might say, haughty. My grandfather was proud of his Arabian. He'd never looked so happy. Evenings, he quickly left the table to go and brush him.

After Chucker came, my grandfather had stopped beating his wife. He drank less. He even stopped pawing my Aunt Jane. You'd think he'd found God.

— Like *reborn Christians*★ you know, explains my mother. He had that kind of *drive*.★

One day, it was a torrid July day, Chucker had been running constantly. His pale coat shone in the sun, wet with sweat. Taking advantage of the fact her father'd turned his back, my mother, who was eight, brought Chucker, as a reward

for his efforts, a pail of water with crushed ice floating in it.
The stallion drank greedily to his fill and collapsed. My grandfather sat on the ground and cried. He caressed Chucker's
forehead, reverently burying his fingers in the horse's black
mane. Like a *pietà*.

In no time, grandpa'd gone back to his old habits. Glasses
of gin. Hands all over Jane. Chair bars broken over Harry's
back. Girls under the window come to chase my grandmother out of her own bed, in the night. Chucker was never men-
tioned again. It was like he'd never existed.

My mother's eyes are swollen. She confides to me: "I
don't know why I did it. *I don't know*★... I think I thought I
was being good."

The coffee with cream isn't going down well and my
heart beats heavily.

We parade into the parlour. Beside me, sure that I am
noting everything down, my Uncle Harry slips me some "useful" information out of the side of his mouth about each visitor. So and so is said not to have said no to my grandfather
when she was fifteen. Such and such worked with him at
Vickers' machine shop in '43; it's with him that Grandpa stole
a barrel of nails. And so on. Between two scoops, he adds that
he'd really like it if I called the character representing him
"Sonny." He sees himself as a "Sonny."

I look at my watch. I smile politely.

Enter Hector Vaillancourt, an erect old man who heads piously towards the casket of the dead man. He kneels on the prie-dieu.

Harry is furious. What does Hector Vaillancourt think gives him the right to set foot in here. This man is said to have extorted three acres of land from my grandfather during the war.

Hector Vaillancourt's arrival causes a small stir among the nearest and dearest. With a firm step, my mother heads in my direction. She clenches her jaw; she does that when she speaks crossly. She taps on my shoulder with a firm index finger and says, "Did you see who just came in? I hope you're noting this all down!"

Monsieur Vaillancourt seems universally detested. He looks like a pleasant self-satisfied second-hand goods dealer.

I remain seated, my shoulders slumped and feet turned in, with the Zellers bag shoved under my chair. With nods, I greet the relatives I recognize. I have a dry mouth, a brown tongue, and, still, heartburn.

It's the last day of exposing the dead man. In an hour, the coffin will be sealed and they'll put him in the ground. Flamboyant Suzy, the practical type, encourages everyone to help themselves to the wreaths. Helen, as circumspect as a woman at the market, sticks her nose in every rose she tears off. My mother gathers carnations: a long-lasting flower good for at least a week. A great-aunt undoes the dedicatory ribbon from a wreath and spreads it out on the coffin lid. She looks at it, pointing to the gold letters: yes, it's reuseable; she could make the word *Noel*, but not *Joyeux*... My Aunt Suzy signals to me to hurry up. I decline.

The bag I have between my legs stinks.

I get up. I go over to say hello to my grandmother; she holds herself up, her hand on the dead man's coffin, near the now stripped-bare wreaths. She holds a spray of daisies, tightly under her arm. She says in a low voice, "*Do your best,*" squeezing my hands.

Quick, a breath of fresh air.

Harry hurries to catch up with me on my way out the door. I'd forgotten the bag of newspapers under the chair. I thank him.

Decisively, almost curtly, I step out.

The sky is cold. I can see my breath in the cold spring air. I almost feel like throwing up. On the steps of the funeral parlour, I hold the smelly sack at arm's length so it won't touch me, and with my eyes, I look around for a garbage can. I don't see one. There is nothing but wide auto routes and abandoned lots.

1995

HELEN WITH A SECRET

for N.G.

I have noticed over the years
that beauty just like happiness
is a frequent occurrence. Not a day goes by
without our entering Paradise, for a moment.

Jorge Luis Borges

Helen goes by train. It takes longer. It will be night when she arrives in Cleveland. In three days, when she has acquitted herself of her visit, she'll go back to Hamilton, back to Bill.

Helen says Gary. She pronounces the name. She drawls the *a*. She draws out the syllables. Gary. To masticate the word. To stretch it. She stares into empty space as she speaks. Gary. The way you doodle while thinking about something else. To think about something else.

She closes her eyes. She lets it pass.

§

Helen holds herself straight. To see me you would never know I am nearly sixty, because I hold myself straight. Well-bred people hold themselves straight. Even after four beers, they remain haughty and proud. When I get to Cleveland, when Eddy sees his mother, she will be looking swell.

Cleveland one more time. For Helen, Ohio is the land of tornadoes, warnings on the radio, streets where infants are picked up by the wind and smashed against cement. In Cleveland, mothers know that children die. With a snap. A clack muffled by the windy fury of the elements.

Ohio is Skip Blanchard.

Ohio is Eddy.

A beer city and the kitchen table with the blue notebook where Helen jots down a word that might be useful, that's Ohio.

§

In 1952, she crosses the Canadian/American border for the first time. A taxi ride Montréal-Burlington. An angry fugue, in a yellow raincoat and rubber rain boots. With a full round stomach. She dozes, purse snuggled tight to her belly where the baby sleeps whom she has already named Gary. The wavering windshield wipers trace a nice image of time moving forward. Hope rocking.

The customs officer thinks she might be Jane Wyman. Helen, charming, bursts out laughing. She says it happens a lot. Helen has a face like the actress's. She tells a little anecdote about that. She expresses herself well. A good storyteller. The customs man is all smiles under the pouring rain.

The taxi driver passes her off as his wife. Big tip for monsieur Laforest. A handful of dollars, proffered eagerly, awkwardly, with gratitude. *God bless you,*★ monsieur Laforest.

§

Today, Helen is taking the train. The train is going too fast. Nothing was made ready for this trip. She didn't have time. She has trouble imagining what awaits her.

In the taxi Montréal–Burlington, in 1952, at the age of sixteen, she had thought of everything.

§

Helen's blue notebook falls open on *Gary-in-the-bedroom*: He's up in the morning/ earlier than everyone else/ stretches his arms, his shoulders,/ his stomach, his thighs./ He stretches his feet./ Take a good look at his hair./ I cut it myself yesterday,/ with a bowl on his head./ We laughed.

The blue notebook is touched up every day. A word weighed, a phrase scanned, a letter retraced, a line cut in two, and put back in place the next day. Every day, a moment of thought for the blue notebook. Cultivating grace. Patience. A beautiful image of time, no, of eternity.

§

Eddy and Helen have a game. Mornings she combs his hair with hair cream. She makes a perfect part, glued in place. When she has finished, she plants a dry little kiss on his nose. Eddy, knowing what comes next, tenses his face and holds his breath. Helen gives him a little slap. Ed giggles. It's always like that. A kiss on the nose, a little tap on the cheek. One balances out the other. And the day starts. Lunch box, notebooks, pencils.

"Bye Mom!"★

The little boy is not in danger. It's not tornado season. The weather's always changing. Everything is normal.

§

Helen's stomach feels upset. She fans herself with a large envelope from the Cleveland Hospital. That's where Eddy's waiting for a new liver. His chances aren't great.

§

In her kitchen in Cleveland she uncaps her beer, eyes riveted on a slogan: *"I'm an alcoholic."*★ She'd hung it up over the sink. She drinks a toast to it. She snorts laughingly, *"I'm an alcoholic."*★ She can't stop laughing. She wipes her mouth with the back of her hand. She bends forward and falls from her chair. She rolls on the floor, killing herself laughing.

Eddy gets home late, saggy walk, stumbling against the doorframe. He pays no attention to his mother draped out on the kitchen floor and heads for his bed where he throws himself, letting go a resonant belch as he falls. The teenager falls asleep with his clothes on. His t-shirt wet with strong-smelling sweat and his jeans worn out on the behind. He fades off, his arms stretched out. He snores. When he's been drinking, he snores.

§

Cleveland's an okay place. Except for the tornadoes. In the middle of America, people call them "God's Finger" or "The Devil's Tail." What's in a name?

§

Helen is crying. Her face is red with greasy sweat and beer. The wind whistles through the door. Dry branches clack against the window pane. Tricycles and chairs are dragged along the ground into the street. The radio is keeping people informed about the cyclone's development. They are recommending that families stay in their basements, everyone together in the southwest corners of their houses. Eddy has slammed the door, saying that nothing, nothing would keep him from going bowling tonight. Helen cries out in distress. Skip has stayed at work. She is huddled, alone, arms crossed, in the southwest corner of the basement.

Helen cries and remembers the first cyclone she saw after arriving in Cleveland. She wasn't yet twenty. She remembers the baby carriage flying through the air and smashing against a cement wall. That's what happens to children on days when there are cyclones. A shiny new baby carriage takes off and in the shock of the impact the metal folds like aluminum paper. The sound of death, a dreadful sound. Nature having its way.

§

Skip Blanchard is a good looking man. Tall. Good with money. That's his best quality. At dinner time, he often orders belt-tightening. Instead of two loaves of bread a week they have to cut back to one and a half. Helen even saw him counting the nails in a new box to make sure he wasn't being cheated at the hardware store.

A note to her parents: "I'm getting married. His name is Skip Blanchard. (He has never heard of Jane Wyman!) I am going to be living in Cleveland. I like it, except for the cyclones."

§

Gary-with-one-shoe-missing: Emptied the Lego boxes./ Found the G.I. Joe we thought was lost./ Looked under the bed./ The mystery continues.

§

Panic. The blue notebook has disappeared. With his feet up on the stool, Skip Blanchard is reading it with a smirk. He mutters, "Gibberish." Helen is relieved. You're right, it's gibberish. Give me back my notebook.

§

Gary-in-heaven: Candles of many colours. A chocolate cake./ Cheeks as round as the Wind,/ we blow together.

§

Skip has disappeared. He has emptied his bank account. He took it all in cash. He sleeps in the Bayou, sheltered by his cash, like a homeless person by his newspapers. While a black man hums "Amazing Grace." The Bayou. The swamp where moss hangs from trees like well-furbished mops. Where crocodiles and snakes glide under the water's flat surface.

He wanted peace and quiet.

§

Bill, I got a letter from my son Eddy. The doctors say he has cirrhosis. He's drunk too much in his life. Like his father Skip. Eddy wasn't violent, though, not at all. Eddy's waiting for a new liver. There isn't much of a chance they will find one for him. I won't be gone for long, Bill.

Bill is fat. I like his eyes. He's a retired policeman. Calm, heavy, steady. Bill, that's my life in Hamilton. Card games in the evenings with him and his friends, who are also retired. A page of the notebook (no longer blue notebooks, but black) in the afternoon while Bill takes his nap. I reread it. I note down a word. I have more than six hundred poems that only I have read. They all start by *Gary-doing-something*. All except one.

Bill's sister says there is something mysterious about me. Tell me about it, Rita.

§

The train rolls along on its iron rails. I am leaving Canada. Like in '52. I am returning to Cleveland. The weather's always changing there. Sun, clouds, rain: fortune's turning wheel. There's a saying: "In Cleveland, if you don't like the weather, wait five minutes." But I've never seen a tornado that only lasted five minutes.

§

Eddy manages on his own. He's a big boy now. He has a bachelor apartment on Preston Street. He leaves the factory when the siren goes off at four. With his work buddies, he goes to the tavern to drink, until ten. He orders a pizza-extra-pepperoni to be delivered and he gets home just ahead of the delivery man. The leftovers (when there are any), get eaten cold at lunch. He's been doing that for years, all on his own, never asking anyone for anything. During his twenties. During his thirties. He always rolled along smoothly.

In a letter, he tells me that doing the same things over and over gives him a feeling of security. Like a solid building that won't topple in a tornado. He says he has never hurt anyone. I know he's telling the truth.

At this hour, he's asleep in the hospital.

I am returning to this city because I have no choice. It is my duty as a mother.

§

Gary-with-the-brown-hair. So much warmth./ So much intensity in his eyes,/ he's all eyes...

§

In her room, Helen lines up her Raggedy Ann dolls, leaning them against each other, Indian file. She is playing bus. Mommy brings her some ice cream. With cookies. Helen is quite the young lady. The pampered one, the spoiled one.

She doesn't like to sew (too finicky) but she sews quite well. She plays the recorder adequately. She is complimented on her drawing. People say she's talented at everything, everything comes easy. She is the darling of the elder sisters, she is their much beribboned doll. "*She gets away with everything.*"★ Barely sixteen. Nothing is refused her. Ice cream, lipstick, pregnancy.

She remains confined to her room. Imprisoned. Hidden from the neighbours. They take her meals up on a tray. She is followed by a doctor, who is in on the secret. Helen spends her days heaving little sighs and drawing skies.

Helen is making plans for her baby. She will call him Gary. She will keep him and he will be American. She will send him to the best colleges in Boston. Mom and Dad, for their part, have arranged for the baby to be adopted.

A late-afternoon taxi. I help myself to all the savings for the holiday at Lake Champlain. Mommy, the cookie jar is empty. Dad, I am falling asleep to the clicking of the wind-shield wipers of Laforest Taxi, snuggled down beside the driver. The metronome is set at rocking cradle. I am making a place for myself in the United States. People will take me for Jane Wyman. I shall ask, and I shall receive.

§

Gary-all-Gary: I bathe him/ in bath bubbles./ I say his name/ pronouncing each syllable slowly./ He splashes the water.

§

In the incubator, the baby's a brown scrawny thing. Sister Irene promises they will call him Gary. Helen explains it is a name that sounds strong. She wants to at least give him that. It will follow him his whole life. Garys are successful at whatever they do. She writes the name on a card so Sister Irene won't forget.

§

For several weeks, Helen lives alone in a room she has rented very close to the hospital. She walks a lot. She recuperates rapidly. Anonymous in the little city. She wanders through the commercial streets with her handbag, with her blue notebook.

Supper is a cheeseburger, a small plate of onion rings and a Coke. She chews slowly. At the corner restaurant, on her usual bench near the window. People passing stop; they think they recognize Jane Wyman. Helen is indifferent to the looks she gets on account of this resemblance. I don't think a lot about Gary. He surely is better off in the nursery where he is, better off than with me. He came to me all shrivelled up. Premature. So now, the baby, that's taken care of.

I had imagined him pink and round. With little Oxford stockings.

In her room, Helen notes down words before falling asleep. The words simmer by themselves while I sleep. When I wake up, I write down a phrase, and it sounds right at first try. Hardly anything has to be reworked. It happens all by itself.

§

Skip Blanchard has appeared.

All man with a square jaw and thick brows. Handsome. Trained in the Marines. Ready to found a family. We settle down in Cleveland. In a house in Cleveland. Skip was born in Cleveland.

Helen doesn't talk much. She's all smiles and coy gestures. A quiet man, this pleases Skip. In her house she lacks nothing. She is married. She has her modern kitchen. She's no longer an *alien*.★

I went a few months without opening the notebook. Skip's newness and the pleasure of getting to know his body made me forget the notebook. A few months. After that, I went back to it. Skip knows nothing. Skip asks nothing. Skip offers nothing. He sweats a lot when he drinks his beer. That's all. It's his metabolism.

Helen takes out the blue notebook again. An hour bent over the words. For the beauty of the little snapshots called Gary. A perfect hour, leaning over my blue notebook.

§

Gary-with-scraped-knee: He has fallen down on the gravel./ He's sobbing heavily./ Blood surges over the skin./ Nothing serious./ I bandage it/ a real mother.

§

After my caesarean in 1956, in my beautiful hospital room at Cleveland Hospital, Skip came to see me, his young wife, to tell me he'd picked the name "Eddy." His son would be called "Eddy." Skip was excited, moved. Smiling and a little out of it, I let him have his way. I willingly give him "Eddy." I practise the new name. The caesarean is a brilliant invention. I fall asleep, I fly away, while this boy is cut out of me. The knife cuts finely under the excess weight to detach it. I carry around scars and that's a bother but it's not like the torture of expelling the child, not like that.

It happened all by itself.

Gary didn't kill me. Eddy won't kill me.

Now I could go back to Montréal. Married. American. Legitimate young mother. In triumph for what I did without them, against their wishes. I could but I don't bother. Always this tiredness in which plans dissolve. He never stops.

§

Gary-at-noon: I pour a glass of milk/ full to the top/ Macaroons that I made myself/ with coconut in them/ as many as he wants./ A white moustache./ Bliss.

§

Skip, his face aged, a gun in his fist, his hand on the cloth bag stuffed with dollars. Peace in the Bayou. Endless bourbon under the tropical heat. Skip sleeps, snuggled like a baby up to the red Santa-Claus bag at the foot of the tree. The smell of ink comes through the cloth. Greenbacks smell good, have the nice smell of the bitter sweat of hands that have laboured. They make you high. A tropical bird trills on a branch. A black fisherman hums a tune that sounds like "Amazing Grace." Skip snores, happy on his heap.

§

In Cleveland Hospital, Eddy lies recumbent, his arms along his sides. In his torpor, in his drugged state, he dreams of his liver: a moving shape, flaccid, a sort of earth black colour. A striped black. Spotted. Unhappy. A painful memory. On weekends, Skip and Helen drink hard. Helen falls asleep on her chair and Skip, the paltry working stiff, has a monstrous angry fit. He beats Eddy with his belt, or he slaps him with his callused hands. Somewhere, in the heart of the father, is the belief that beating will toughen Eddy up, make of him a man nothing can hurt. Eddy cannot imagine life any other way.

The next day, Helen puts a band aid on Eddy's wound. You keep your mouth shut.

At times like that, Helen pays attention to signs. A new idea can come up at any minute for the blue notebook. A word. A gesture. A utensil. Something to connect to the name of Gary.

§

Gary-in-the-peaceful-water: His navy blue bathing suit,/ I spent a lot on it./ The total joy in the picture./ We will fish for mini-trouts/ as dusk falls.

§

Little Helen has emptied the cookie jar. Papa and Mama wanted to give Gary to the orphanage. Erase him. Like a mistake. Helen has fled to the States. She will keep her baby and make a famous man of him. I have great expectations for Gary. Sometimes, it frightens me.

§

No doubt about it. Skip has drunk away his money. Thousands of dollars painfully amassed over some twenty-five years. Nothing for Eddy. Nothing for Helen. No doubt about it.

The F.B.I. came to say Skip's remains had been found, in Louisiana, in a cabin he paid cash for. They identified him by his teeth and the plastic he had on him. His skull has a hole out the top from a bullet that entered through his mouth.

§

Helen has polished *Gary-on-third-base*: A baseball uniform./ Of clean finely striped cloth./ The smell of green soap on the back of his neck./ He keeps his foot on the base./ I stop breathing when someone hits/ the ball.

§

Helen gives up Gary, that little crumpled and rubbery thing. Helen leaves him in the incubator. She is overcome by a sudden tiredness at the thought of nursing him. She is overcome with a sudden tiredness thinking of her hopes for Gary. The Boston college. Prizes for excellence. Degrees. She softens at every recollection. Sister Irene places the boy in the orphanage. It isn't Helen's business any more. The State of Vermont takes care of everything.

Inquisitive women come and peek around the hospital curtain. People say the actress Jane Wyman has just had a baby. There's nothing in the papers.

Melancholic, Helen often snivels. With her fingers on her lips, she moans like a hostess who has just seen her soufflé fall as she takes it out of the oven.

Sister Irene brings her a blue notebook. To write down your future plans, she says.

§

A first poem *Gary-fed-with-yellow-milk*: Each mouthful my treasure takes./ Suckling with white gaze./ My bundle is heavy./ I engorge it with nurturing/ I am left full.

Helen writes without thinking.

Sister Irene congratulates her. *It's Dickinson, but earthier!* Sister Irene enthuses.

Helen leaves the hospital. Purse and blue notebook.

§

Skip Blanchard in his cabin in Louisiana. Bought on the spot. He throws back his bourbon. He guards his sack of dollars like a wild dog. Armed. Alone. A heavy thud rings through the swamp. Skip rotting somewhere in the Bayou until the odour of decaying carcass and the mad buzzing of flies attract the attention of a fisherman who happens by. One imagines a laid-back Black man gliding his boat along with easy strokes of a pole. He is humming "Amazing Grace."

§

Bill, as soon as I've seen Eddy, I'll be back in Hamilton. Cleveland's not good for me.

§

Gary-at-school: I am dying today./ He is clean./ He is so handsome/ for his first day./ I have combed his hair,/ a straight shiny part./ He is a little man./ He is my heart of hearts./ I wait all day/ for him to come back.

§

I pace up and down in the corridor. I am trying to gain time. Behind my back, the doctors are watching me, I know it. They see this old woman with dyed black hair clasping her shiny leather purse. They see my hunched back. They imagine my skinny legs under the turquoise pants. My bony shoulders that stick out under my beige shirt. The stretched skin over my swollen stomach. My stomach full of water. I am not my older sisters' little doll any more. The pampered, spoiled kid. I am no longer Jane Wyman for the American Customs' agents. I no longer have breasts and my lipstick traces thinner and thinner lips. Little crayoned lines. I don't know why I draw these old lady's lips on myself.

I stayed a long time in the corridor, opposite his room's door. For a moment, I felt Eddy's nearness. That made me happy because I thought it might be enough: being there in the corridor without going in to see him, without talking to him, without seeing how he was going to look dead, because I know that he is going to die. Who would give his liver to Eddy? It's a lottery. I don't come from a line of winners.

I have uncapped a lot of bottles in my life. It's only very recently that I have been able to limit my daily dose. Never more than four. Eddy always saw me with a bottle in my hand. And his father drank, too. For sure we were bad examples.

Eddy looks puffy. Waxy. The small beer of his childhood is oozing through his pores. It wells up out of him. His forehead is balding. Receding like Skip's. His skin is pale under his black whiskers. I should have written him. A word of encouragement. Something sweet. A card with good wishes inside, that would have made him happy. Or even some chocolates; they sell them in the boutique on the ground floor. Eddy likes chocolate. If I back out slowly, without a sound, he won't wake up.

He says, "*Ma?*" I say, "*It's me, Ed.*" If he tells me he is going to die, I'll tell him everybody dies some time; that will make him feel better.

We don't talk. He is crying a little but his face is expressionless. I want to disappear. I want to go and take my train. I want to go back to Hamilton, to be with Bill. I look at Eddy. I smile to raise his morale.

I think about the blue notebooks. It's all I think about.

§

Gary-with-five-spots: Fair skin has an odour/ all its own./ The youthful down. / Little round café-au-lait spots on the left hip/ My eyes run over his lower back/ I breathe him in.

§

Gary didn't kill me. Eddy won't kill me.

When I get back to Hamilton, I'll ask Bill to send a little money. Some chocolates or flowers. For Eddy.

§

It still inspires me to think about Gary. I immediately see the luminous child of my notebooks. He's perfect. As unassailable as the gold trim on an icon. And noone could find the exact spot where the word nape is in my blue notebooks, like I can. Or the word boat. The word Indian. The word baseball.

It's with my notebooks that I talk to the everlasting. My words resonate up there with the stars.

I know what's on every page. I created it all. I could destroy them in a second. I know they tremble before me. It is through me that they exist. I am a huge presence for the multitude of little Garys. Due to the kindness of my heart, my infinite kindness, I let them live.

§

Helen pushes up her earring on her right lobe. The springs are loose and it keeps slipping down.

I have all the paperwork. Eddy is laid out in his case. I am going back to Hamilton with him. I will introduce him to Bill. I will tell him Eddy was always such a sweet kid. I will say he was a solitary kid who liked pizza. He never bothered anybody. He never did any harm to anyone. We will have a mass said. He will have his little marble plaque and his bouquet of flowers.

Eddy died the night I arrived. His kidneys gave up. They would have had to transplant his entire insides.

I tied a scarf around my hair. I put on my sunglasses. I signed the papers.

§

Fifteen years ago, in the train station before coming back to Canada to live with Bill, I opened my worn notebook and I wrote: *He-who-dies-three-times*: He is killed in a plane crash./ He is killed in a car crash./ He is dead in a boat accident./ Who remembers all his names?

I don't like this page. It irritates me. Gary's name is missing. Caught up in my writing, I forgot it.

Gary.

He made a tragedy of my life. Were it not for him, I'd be a faded fat American woman, telling the same old tornado stories over and over. But somebody already said about me, and I remember this clearly. "*Helen, you're a woman with a secret.*"★ I am a woman with a secret.

Gary.

I will carry the emptiness all my life. I will remain as faithful to it as an oft-repeated prayer. I will die with this pain and I will return with a desire so great, so strong, as to make me luminous. That will be my glory. I see myself. I am glorious.

And they want me to cry now. Because I have my health, they want me to cry. They want me to release into nothingness the thing that makes sense of my days.

They want me to tell my secret.

No thanks.

1994

NOTE

The short story "Fallow Ground" was originally commissioned by TVOntario. It was initially written for adolescents learning French as a second language.